BLOOD LINE

BLOOD LINE

A Gabe Wager Mystery

REX BURNS

WALKER AND COMPANY
NEW YORK

First published in the United States of America in 1995 by Walker Publishing Company, Inc.

Published simultaneously in Canada by Thomas Allen & Son Canada, Limited, Markham, Ontario

Library of Congress Cataloging-in-Publication Data
Burns, Rex
Blood line / a Gabe Wager mystery / Rex Burns.
p.   cm.
ISBN 0-8027-3256-9
I. Title.
PS3552.U7325B57   1995
813′ .54—dc20   94-48329
                                    CIP

Printed in the United States of America
2 4 6 8 10 9 7 5 3 1

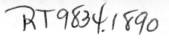

To Pat and Dale

1

EACH FAMILY HAS its whore and its thief. It was a saying Detective Gabe Wager had heard as a kid when the doings of one relative or another had generated shocked and angry whispers among the women who kept track of each other's nephews and nieces: *Cada familia tiene su puta y su ladrón.* But not all families had their cop, a fact that Wager and his relatives had been forced to live with for many years. So many that, eventually, he no longer paid much attention to the guarded politeness and the corny jokes from those who called him Cousin. Since he no longer let it bother him, he was surprised to discover that anyone else in his family still had trouble with it.

"He won't talk to me. He says I'm the aunt of a cop."

The voice on the telephone quavered with some half-controlled emotion, but Wager—rubbing his eyes and trying to ignore the whining clatter of computer printers, the sharp outbursts from police radios sitting in their desk chargers, the incessant electronic chirp from one or another of the surrounding telephones—didn't know if his aunt's emotion was anger at her son for being stubborn or at him for being what a social worker might call an unfit role model. "Tell him he's the cousin of a cop. Tell him it's a family disease."

While he talked, he initialed the last page of a thick report he was packaging up for Assistant District Attorney Kolagny. The man should have gone into private practice long ago, like the rest of the ADAs who let the state pay them to learn enough criminal law so they could hang out their own shingles. But Kolagny was a slow learner—the kind who wouldn't be able to feed himself without a guaranteed paycheck. Wager figured that in his own way Kolagny was serving the common weal by staying off the unemployment rolls. But it still meant that Wager had to send up four-square cases that even Kolagny couldn't lose. And that called for extra work, and it wasn't always successful.

"Gabriel, please don't make no jokes. I'm so worried—I ain't never seen him like this. He's . . . frightened. But he won't tell me why. He won't go to school, he won't go to work, and he don't even go out. He won't talk on the phone unless I tell him who it is. And these people keep calling—they hang up without saying nothing when I answer."

Kolagny could even lose this one: a domestic with victim and assailant wearing the same blood, and which should take the ADA a hell of a lot less time in court than it took Wager to write up. Not only was the gun smoking, the blood was still smoking when the patrol officers came through the door. Even the perp had been equally hot, a wife who had discovered what a shotgun could do to Mr. Slusser's personality, not to mention his belly, and had insisted on telling Wager and every other officer in earshot that the low-life son of a bitch deserved what he got, that she didn't give a goddamn who Miranda was or anybody else, and that if the shit-sucker wasn't dead by the time he reached the hospital, she, Mrs. Slusser, would by God do it again. Even Kolagny should be able to handle that.

"Maybe he'll talk to you, Gabe. Maybe what he needs is a man to talk to." "He" was cousin Julio, sixteen—seventeen?—

somewhere around there. Old enough to have a driver's license, but young enough to still be in high school and trouble, both. "All right, Aunt Louisa. I'll come over. . . ." The radio mounted in its desk charger popped with the code number for homicide and the familiar request for "any homicide detective." Wager covered the telephone speaker and, his aunt's voice buzzing in one ear, replied with his call number. The dispatcher's precise voice gave him an address that he jotted down quickly, replying with an automatic "ten-four." Aunt Louisa's voice was saying "Gabe? Gabe?"

"I'll be over this evening, Aunt Louisa." He shrugged into his sport coat and holstered the radio as he talked. "I really will."

His aunt was saying something about not wanting to bother Wager, and he let her apology go on for a few seconds before interrupting. "It's all right, Aunt Louisa." She had got what she wanted, and now she had to pretend that he could have said no—that it was Wager who had called up and insisted he come by and talk to Julio instead of her calling to ask a favor. "I should get off around five and I'll be over after that. . . . It's no problem, really. . . . It's all right." She was still making "You're really sure?" noises when he said he had to go and hung up.

Initialing the route slip on the Slusser file, Wager quickly slid the packet into a mailer and dropped it in the interdepartmental delivery box on his way to the elevator. Five minutes later, he was driving up the ramp from the police headquarters garage into the traffic of Cherokee Street.

"WE GOT A positive on him." The uniformed officer didn't look at either Wager or the small, dark shape in the striped T-shirt and frayed, cutoff denims. It had been flung like trash into weeds and chokecherry bushes that had grown up around the broken foundations marking the remains of the demolished

Stapleton housing project. The weedy concrete pads, the low mounds of overgrown rubble, the strips of broken sidewalk that led nowhere reminded Wager of an old cemetery. And, in a way, that's what it had become. "John Erle Hocks. One of the kids that found him knew him, and his mother came down for a positive ID. That's her over in the car."

It wasn't routine to bring a relative to the crime scene; the procedure called for identification in the morgue where, even before the cosmetics of an undertaker, the dead were given a little more dignity. "You brought her down here?"

"No, Detective Wager. We did not bring her down here." The patrolman's silver name tag said L. Minks, and he let the disgust in his tone sink in for a moment. "She came down here herself. Took a goddamn bus. One of the kids who found him told somebody who called her."

"All right. Witnesses?"

"My partner's still canvassing." He nodded toward a row of bungalows that showed their dilapidated back fences far across the neglected stretch. The steady rush of traffic, invisible behind a tall wooden sound barrier, came like a noisy stream off I-25. A block to the east loomed an old brick school building built before World War II, three-story, square, and gloomy. It was now a private home for mentally retarded juveniles.

Harry Gebauer and his team from the forensics lab, whose radios monitored the homicide frequency, had arrived at about the same time as Wager and were now stringing yellow barrier tape around the site and trying to determine where people had walked after the body had been discovered. The flash of a strobe light made a dim pulse in the midday sun. Behind the line of marked and unmarked police cars at the distant curb, an ambulance waited, its crew leaning against the orange-and-white truck and staring toward the weeds. A white Honda Civic skidded to a halt behind the ambulance, and a familiar black T-shirt hurried through the tall grass toward the cheery yellow tape:

Gargan, ace crime reporter for the *Denver Post*. Wager turned his back to the bustling figure.

"One round to the back of the neck." Minks stared at his clipboard as if reading the words. "Came out the top of his skull."

"Any gang symbols?" It was what you asked now when children were shot.

"None I saw. I didn't go through his pockets."

"That's good." The less a victim or site was disturbed, the better the lab people liked it. That was repeated to every uniformed cop a dozen times a year, but more often than not they poked around anyway. Everybody wanted to play detective. Wager copied down the few notes the officer had—the names of the kids who found the body, the time, the fact that no witnesses had been located. And probably wouldn't be; the area was almost deserted during the day and more so at night, and from the heavy appearance of the torso and its twisted, skinny legs, Wager figured the body had been here since last night at least. Bodies did that with time: tended to sag into the earth, to conform to the shape of the ground they lay on. It was as if they wanted to find refuge by sinking out of sight. "I'll see what the mother has to say."

"All yours."

She was a gaunt woman with high cheekbones and dark eyes that stared unseeing through the iron grille behind the patrol car's front seat and on out the windshield. She did not turn her head to look when Wager showed his badge, and he stood in the sun at the open car door. It was a way of observing the formality and privacy of her grief. "Can you tell me when you saw your son last, Mrs. Hocks?"

Her answer wasn't a word but a moan, the kind made by someone who hurts badly in their sleep.

"Mrs. Hocks?"

"Uh-uh."

An insect zinged into the shade of the car and batted itself against the windshield before finding an open window and zipping away. Wager felt the late August sun press hotly on his neck and shoulders. "Mrs. Hocks, we want to find who did this. We need your help for that, so I've got to ask you some questions. I'd appreciate you trying to answer them, OK?"

The staring brown eyes closed slowly, and she nodded.

"When did you see your son last?"

"Las' night. After supper." The whisper barely made it past her dry lips.

Wager caught the eye of one of the lounging ambulance attendants. "You got any water in your vehicle? Something she can drink?"

The attendant looked surprised, as if he were really seeing the woman for the first time. "Yeah—hang on." He trotted back to his ambulance and returned with a can of 7-UP. "It's cold— we keep it in the medicine reefer."

"Thanks." Wager opened it and handed it to the woman, who sat with it in her hand. "Take a drink, Mrs. Hocks. Drink up."

She followed his directions.

The attendant, a ponytail and thick glasses, hovered. "She need anything? She a relative?"

"Mother. No. Thanks."

"Give me a call if she does."

Wager nodded. The attendant wandered back to his ambulance and said something to his partner, who glanced their way. Then they stared across the open space as the three lab men measured, took notes, photographed, picked up things, and put them in plastic Baggies.

"Las' night. After supper."

Wager nodded. The woman's voice was stronger now. She'd probably start wailing soon. Give way to tears and sobs and even screams. You wanted to get your information before that happened. "Did he say where he was going?"

She shook her head. "Went out on his bicycle. Was still light. And then he jus' didn't come home."

"Did you file a missing persons report, Mrs. Hocks?"

She shook her head. "I kep' figuring he'd come home. I went on to sleep—I go to work early and John Erle, he likes to stay out late summer nights. . . ." Her voice almost broke, but something inside managed to stifle what she was feeling, and Wager had the sense that this wasn't one of those women who would wail in public but who would hold in her grief, live with it silently.

"Do you have any idea who might have wanted to kill him?"

"No! Ain't nobody want to kill him! Who want to kill a little boy like that?"

"How old was he, Mrs. Hocks?"

"Was." She gripped the wrinkling can with both hands. The dark skin of her large knuckles paled. "Thirteen. Be fourteen ten December. Thirteen and a half." A shuddering breath. "Tha's all."

"Can you give me the names of some of his friends, kids he hung around with?"

Her brown eyes blinked, and she drew her mind back from wherever it had gone. "Londe. That's his best friend. They some others—I don't know. . . ."

"What school did your son go to?"

"The middle school. Cole Middle School."

"Is there anything you can think of that might help us, Mrs. Hocks?"

"No."

"Is it possible your son was in a gang? Or thinking about joining one?"

"Gang? John Erle? He wasn't in no gang! He wasn't one of them!"

"Yes, ma'am." Despite the woman's denials, her son's death looked like a gang assassination, and at thirteen John Erle was prime gang bait. But Wager wasn't going to argue with her. He asked a few more questions, trying to get more names, more places John Erle hung out, more leads to people who might know more than she did herself about her son's real life. But she didn't have much to add: She clerked at a convenience store, six-thirty to three in the afternoon, a lot of times she worked an extra shift in the evenings or part-time as a janitor's assistant. John Erle was her only son, and a real smart boy and a good one, and wouldn't be in no gang. Always did good in school without even trying, seemed like. He had two younger sisters, Coley and Jeanette. Their father was long gone, left somewhere down in Texas when she and the kids had moved up to Denver four years ago, looking for the better life. Wager got her address and telephone, where the girls went to school, and finally closed his notebook. "The officers will give you a ride home, Mrs. Hocks. Is there anybody we can call to stay with you for a while?"

"I be all right."

"It would be good for you to have somebody around."

"I be all right."

"Yes, ma'am." Wager said good-bye and headed across the deserted fragments of sidewalk for the taped-off area.

The forensics team had finished, and two of them stood comparing notes while Gebauer toted his metal detector back to the trunk of their vehicle. He held up a labeled Baggie for Wager to see. "Found the slug. Looks like a thirty-two."

Wager peered at the twisted wad. Although its nose was splayed by impact with bone and dirt, the base of the bullet was still intact enough for a ballistics test. "Good. If the killer's dumb enough to keep the weapon, and if we're smart enough to find the killer, we might have a case." But more and more, gang shooters tended to use throwaway guns—cheap, small-caliber weapons that couldn't be traced to whoever pulled the trigger.

"Yeah, well, I leave that to you, Gabe; my fun's ended and yours is just beginning."

The ambulance attendants were waved over, and it was time for Wager to inspect the victim, to get the preliminary forensic reports on the body and site before the body was removed, and to draw his own sketch of the crime scene that would provide accurate memory if he were called upon months from now to testify in court.

AUNT LOUISA'S HOUSE was one of the small bungalows just off 38th Avenue in District One, the northwest quadrant of Denver. It was mostly one story, though sometime in the past a couple of attic rooms had been added by poking a pair of flat dormers through the roof to get a little more space. The one with the yellow light glowing dimly behind the small windows was probably Julio's room. Wager pulled his Camaro into the driveway and stood a minute before climbing the three wooden stairs up to the porch.

He had spent the long afternoon following up the patrolman's neighborhood contacts and rapping on doors that, for one reason or another, hadn't answered to the uniformed officer. No one heard or saw anything, and Wager would have been surprised if they had. The residents in the single row of small houses said all they ever heard was noise from the highway, and the staff members at the home for the mentally retarded said their doors and windows were always closed and the building secured at night against neighborhood vandalism. Wager had put off talking to John Erle's sisters, figuring they had enough to handle today. And besides, he was exhausted. A new murder—especially a kid's—always left him feeling weary. What he did not feel like was playing the Dutch uncle to a reluctant teenager. But a promise was a promise.

Aunt Louisa met him at the door, a square shape in a black dress with her gray hair pulled back into a bun. She had worn black ever since Uncle Julius died, over ten years ago, and Wager—who had stopped going to the family gatherings and hadn't seen her in almost two years—tried to pretend he didn't notice the new lines of deep worry on her forehead or the sharper lines beside her mouth. They gave her a bitter look that he did not associate with his memory of the woman, and that made him feel a little twinge of something at having avoided his family for so long. "Gabe—come in!" She gave him an *abrazo*, wrapping him in the thin aroma of some unnamed perfume or soap or lotion that brought back a tangle of almost forgotten feelings and sharpened the sense of so much time passing between what he remembered and what he now saw. They talked for a few minutes, Aunt Louisa urging him to have a cup of coffee and some of the small almond cookies she had lined up formally on a plate. "I'll go get Julio. He's just upstairs."

Wager sipped at the coffee, savoring its thickness and aroma—his aunt and his mother had always challenged each other at coffee making—and listened to her footsteps up the stairs and across the creaky floor above. Then there was a long silence punctuated by a rising mumble that suddenly and self-consciously dropped into another silence. Then the ceiling creaked again, and his aunt's steps came heavily down the stairs. The lines beside her mouth were deeper, but she forced a smile. "He'll be down in a couple minutes, Gabe. He was sleeping, you know?" She added, "I hope you're not in no hurry."

Wager shook his head. "The coffee's good, Aunt Louisa." He searched for something to talk about besides his afternoon's work and remembered his cousin Donna's wedding—her third, he thought—and asked about that. His aunt was glad to tell him, including histories of the first two husbands and dropping a few names that Wager recognized and a lot that he didn't. But he nodded and made the right kind of sounds in the right places, and let her words fill the space until they heard the sullen thud of Julio's heels on the stairs.

The young man paused, eyeing Wager like a nervous cat. Julio had grown half a foot and now had some weight across the shoulders; a hint of dark hairs promised a mustache, and his arms were gaining the thickness of a man's though they didn't yet have the ropy muscles of hard use and repetitive labor.

"You want some coffee, Julio? Your cousin Gabe's having some coffee."

He shrugged, which his mother took for a yes and went quickly to the kitchen for another saucer and cup; Wager saw in the gesture a remnant of the younger boy Julio had been after his father died: sulky and stubborn, wanting something but too proud to admit that he needed anything from anyone.

"Hello, Julio." Wager stood and held out a hand, man-to-man. "Your mother thinks we should talk."

"Talk about what?"

"She's afraid you're in trouble. She's worried about you."

"I ain't in no trouble."

"I'm not the one saying you are. It's your mother who is. Remember her? She's the one brought you into this world. Changed your diapers. Kept a roof over your head after your dad died."

Aunt Louisa came back with a cup and served her son, tilting a dollop of milk into the coffee the way she knew he liked it. "I got to go next door for a little bit. You two excuse me, OK?"

Wager stood and thanked her again for the coffee; Julio remained sitting and frowned at the steam rising from his cup. When the woman had closed the door behind her, Wager sat and munched another of the carefully arranged almond cookies. "How you doing in school?"

"Fine. I'm doing fine."

Wager took another bite. "Your mother tells me you've been missing a lot lately."

A shrug.

"Well, you're right—it's your life; you're the one that's responsible for it—good, bad, or indifferent."

"What's the point in school, man? I ain't going to college—I don't need all that shit they talk about."

Wager didn't have the heart to argue with that. In fact, Julio was repeating the words that he had used, too, before he quit school and joined the Marine Corps with his mother's half-relieved, half-worried blessing and her signature on the age-waiver form. "Hey, I didn't finish high school, either, and, look, it didn't hurt me: Now I'm the family cop."

For the first time, Julio looked directly at him, defensiveness replaced by the puzzlement of whether Wager was joking or not.

"So what about your job? Your mother told me you have this job with the Youth Opportunity Program. What kind of work they have you doing?"

"Construction."

He waited for more, but Julio turned back to reading the wallpaper.

"So, they teaching you a trade? Carpentry? Concrete work?"

"No. I quit."

Wager took another cookie and nudged the plate toward Julio, who studied the blobs of pale pink and white and green for a moment and then picked one up.

"Why?"

"They didn't have me doing nothing but cleaning up crap—picking up lumber and plastic and crap after the workmen. So I quit."

"And now you stay around the house all the time and don't go out at all."

"Yeah. That's what I do."

Wager started to ask him who he was hiding from, but the jangle of the telephone, loud in the still house, interrupted. Julio stiffened, brown eyes wide as he stared toward the small table that held the old-fashioned dial telephone; Wager picked it up. "Hello?"

"Julio? Where you been, man? We want to talk to you."

"Who's this?"

The voice, male and young sounding, paused. "This Julio?"

"I asked you first."

The line clicked dead. Wager put the handset in its cradle. Julio had seemed to shrink, the half-eaten bit of pink cookie held between fingers that were still slender with boyhood. His dark eyes watched Wager intently.

"It's whoever's after you."

He said nothing.

"You in a gang, Julio?"

"No."

"Sometimes it's hard not to be, neighborhood like this. Not a real member, maybe. Just a friend of a friend who is. Know a little bit of what's going down, maybe say the wrong thing by accident, give some people the wrong idea."

"That's not it, man—I'm not in a gang!" He stood abruptly, clattering his coffee cup and sloshing liquid into its saucer. "Just leave me alone, you hear? Leave me alone—get out of my goddamn house and leave me the fuck alone!" His feet thudded up the stairs.

WAGER HAD WAITED until Aunt Louisa came back and then told her what happened and tried to calm her worry with the promise to try again.

"I don't know who else to talk to, Gabe. His teachers, they don't tell me nothing except he should come back to school. The priest tells me to pray. His boss at his job, Mr. Tarbell, says he don't know why Julio quit. He was doing a good job, Mr. Tarbell said, and he can come back but he can't hold the job open for too much longer. I just don't know. . . ."

It had gone on for another half hour—wet, repetitious, and nasal—and Wager had felt the stirrings of anger at Julio not only for what he was putting his mother through but also for what promised to develop into a major drain on Wager's time. He didn't need it, he didn't want it; but it was *la familia*, and there was no way out when somebody like Aunt Louisa asked for help. That's what he was telling Elizabeth Voss as they divided up a double order of spaghetti and drained the carafe of red wine into their glasses.

She preferred wine with her food—"Pasta and beer? Gabe, how can your stomach do that?"—and, after a while, Wager had come to like it too. Good thing, because the couple of years they had spent together so far had shown him that Elizabeth wasn't going to change. Not that she prided herself on being stubborn, but she had lived long enough to make up her mind about a few things, as well as to understand there was a lot she didn't know. She had, after all, a life of her own that included divorce, a career in commercial real estate, a son now in college, and four years on the Denver City Council. In fact, Wager met her at the scene of a riot in District Two; she had been the only councilperson with the guts to show up and, despite Wager's warning, had made an effort to calm the situation. The attempt failed, and Elizabeth blamed herself more than the rioters. But out of that guilt began a series of interviews and meetings to learn a lot more about the city she spoke for. One of those meetings had been with Wager, to thank him as well as to pick his brain. When he asked her if she would like to see Denver from a cop's perspective, she said yes. A patrol car, when the city's quiet at night, is a good place to talk; it was also one of the few times in his life that Wager had felt comfortable enough to talk. At first he thought it was because they were in a police car, but then he realized it was the woman. Elizabeth asked questions, she listened, she wanted to know. And not just about the city and its people. After a while, he realized he even enjoyed talking with her.

"Do you believe he's not in a gang?" Elizabeth, along with the rest of the city council members, had been faced with the rapidly growing gang problems in Denver and its neighboring cities. The Hocks murder was only more evidence of the pervasive violence and the younger age of victims. For the past few years, summer nights had been marked with drive-by shootings, and every Saturday night registered half a dozen reports of gunfire. Children and teenagers, mostly from the Hispanic and black neighborhoods of Districts One and Two, were routinely checked into Denver General's emergency room—the Knife and Gun Club, medics called it—with a variety of wounds. Schools had been trying desperately to be neutral territories by banning gang-style clothing, holding shakedowns for weapons, using dogs to sniff for drugs, expelling armed kids, and establishing uniformed patrols in the halls and on the grounds. Wager figured that pretty soon the teachers would be striking for flak jackets and combat pay. It was, Elizabeth believed, the legacy of Reagan and that era's selfish callousness; Wager thought there was more to it than that, and they'd had some pretty sharp disputes over it. "His mother said he doesn't wear colors; I didn't see any tattoos. But that doesn't mean some gang members aren't after him." Wager shook his head when the waitress asked if they would like more wine.

"Why would they be?" The little spark came into Elizabeth's hazel eyes, a signal to Wager that the issue of gangs was pushing that quick temper.

"It's one of the things I have to find out." He didn't feel like an argument, so he didn't tell her about that voice on the telephone asking for Julio. But he wasn't going to have someone else, even Elizabeth, tell him how to do his job. "And I'm not going to say he is in one if I don't know that for a fact."

She apparently heard something in his voice. "Well, you're right, of course. You shouldn't jump to conclusions, nor should I. But," she added, unwilling to roll over and die, "I wouldn't be surprised if a gang wasn't at the bottom of it."

Neither would Wager, and, mouth too full of spaghetti to speak, he nodded. After all, it wasn't just Wager's belief about the causes of the gang problem that had Elizabeth on edge: it was the upcoming campaign for reelection and the constant harping on crime that filled the almost nightly citizen's meetings. The elderly were terrified for themselves, the parents worried about their children, neighborhoods that had not yet been invaded were afraid of getting hit by the violence they read about in the newspapers, and even some gang members—for whatever reasons, and Wager had his beliefs about that too—spoke against the rising rate of death and mayhem. He had asked Elizabeth why she wanted to run for city council again, and her answer had been one he understood: You don't quit just because things get tough.

She was a good woman.

3

WAGER'S PROBLEM WITH Julio was quickly pushed aside by the death of a patrolman in the neighboring city of Aurora. The story went around that he was shot while making a routine traffic stop. Like everybody else in the department, Wager had heard the latest FBI statistics: one officer killed in the line of duty every three or four days, 50,000 officers assaulted every year, 19,000 injured severely enough to file a report, and who knew how many who didn't want to bother with the paperwork. In fact, academy trainees were told in the Safety Procedures and Techniques class that they should expect to be assaulted or should get out of the business. Federal agencies provided other statistics, too: 91 percent of all officer deaths resulted from shootings, 70 percent occurred during "routine patrol," only 27 percent of the officers killed had a chance to shoot back, the average length of service of officers killed was eleven years. The number of civilians carrying concealed firearms was estimated at between one and four million, and now some damned fool of a state legislator had introduced a bill allowing Colorado citizens to carry concealed handguns legally and without a license.

But none of those facts and none of those words could say what it felt like to call the wife and children of a friend and fellow worker to tell them that Daddy wouldn't be coming home to-night—that they were now widow and orphan and eligible for all the benefits thereof, as well as the flag off the coffin.

Though neither Wager nor many of the members of the Denver Police Department knew the Aurora cop, it was still like a death in the family. One of those third or fourth cousins whose name you might have heard, or maybe you'd met someone who drank coffee with him and had talked fishing or schools for the kids. It was also a reminder to everyone of things that were usually shoved to the back of your mind. So a sadness hung in the air of the Police Administration Building, and everybody seemed to be doing their work with their minds somewhere else, as if they had lost something and were trying to remember where it was. There was a hint of unusual gentleness when people talked to each other, an implied sharing of family hurt, and—beneath it all—the question: What mistake did he make? What mistake could I make?

It would be nothing like the hurt and anger felt in the Aurora PD, of course. But the Denver patrols—especially in the bordering Districts Two and Three, as well as the new District Five that took in the site of the Denver International Airport—would be extra alert as the officers studied every vehicle that remotely matched the description of the killer's car.

Wager, aware of the emotion around him, tried to keep his mind focused on the morning's work: another pass through the facts and guesses concerning John Erle. He had interviewed the boy's two sisters, and they had given him a couple of names but little more; at a shy eight and nine, they were distant from the life of their thirteen-year-old brother, picking up only that part of his world that came home with him. Mrs. Hocks still swore that her son was not involved with a gang, that he was a good boy and too smart; but Wager's interviews with kids in Hocks's neighborhood had turned up a variety of rumors, a few of which might be true. According to them, Hocks was being recruited by the AK Bloods or maybe the Deuce Nine Crips or perhaps the CC Riders, he was either a full-fledged member or only a wanna-be who needed to prove he had heart, he was maybe peddling crack, he might have sold bonk to some Inca Boys who thought they were getting real crack, some said he had "disrespected" the Deuce Nine Crips or the CMG Bloods by marking over their territorial graffiti. To find out what was true, what was the boy's own imaginative bragging, what were only the guesses of the other kids, would take more interviews, some luck, and somebody who knew something and was willing to talk to a cop. That last, the most important, was the most difficult. In Hocks's neighborhood, cops were generally hated, and damn few were trusted. Certainly in the black neighborhoods, Wager and every other policeman was seen as an enemy, not just for their uniforms but because of their skin colors, too. But of course the word "racism" couldn't be used to describe that attitude. Nonetheless, he thought wryly, it wasn't much different from the way his own Hispanic *hermanos* thought of him.

Overcoming that kind of attitude would be helped by having a black homicide detective. But one hadn't yet moved up to take the place of Armstrong, who had left almost a year ago to join the Portland, Oregon, PD. That left Wager and others relying on people like Sergeant Blainey, himself an African-American and resident of District Two. So Wager telephoned the dispatcher and set up a meet with the patrolman. Then he pushed his name across the location board to the On Patrol column and took the elevator down to the chill, stale air of the basement garage.

IF BLAINEY HAD changed at all in the years Wager had known the man, it was only to get a larger neck size. His face, round as a pumpkin, glistened with perspiration as it did summer and winter, and the same frown of concentration wrinkled the dark flesh between his eyebrows. "We use to have our gangs, too, Gabe. I recollect a few good fights with some of you west side Chicanos—hell, high school football games, that was the time for mixing things up a little back of the stands, you know?"

Wager nodded as if he remembered jolly high school fights, and picked at the nutty bumps under the opaque glaze of his donut. He wasn't quite sure what they were, and he hadn't really wanted to order anything, but Blainey—who seemed to eat whenever he got out of his cruiser—had urged it on Wager. It was, he said, a gift of the diner's owner, who liked to have uniformed cops stop by; he was about the only one along this stretch of East 26th who hadn't been robbed, and he figured it was because the hoods weren't sure when a cop would be sitting here. "I ain't about to tell him it's because he don't have nothing worth robbing." Blainey grinned, the silver of a repaired molar glinting far back in his mouth. "He wouldn't believe me. But then the robbers wouldn't neither, so maybe he's right."

"Have you heard anything more about Hocks?"

"Heard he been seen hanging around Big Ron. Which I guess makes him dumber than Ron is."

"A wanna-be Blood? That's definite?"

Blainey nodded. "Little girl my youngest daughter goes to Sunday school with told her. I talked to her and she swears it's true. Saw Hocks and Big Ron sitting over in Morrison Park. Says they looked like they be talking a little business. She described both of them good—knows them both too. And got no reason to lie." Blainey added, "That little girl's only ten years old, Gabe. Already knows a dope deal when she sees one going down. Swear to God, you'd think we lived in Washington, DC, or Detroit or one of them hellholes."

Big Ron Tipton was one of those names that had been around the District Two station so long that it seemed like it was on the duty roster. He was still in his twenties, but, including his juvenile record, he had at least two decades of contact cards in his file. The last Wager had heard was that the man was a Blood associate as well as a small-time crack peddler. Big and dumb—mentally handicapped in some way—he was supposed to be working his way toward the inner ring of longtime members who made up the core of most established gangs. Norm Fullerton, who gave briefings to the police divisions on the latest gang profile, had said that the black gangs usually weren't as organized as the white ones. Those tended to have presidents and vice-presidents, treasurers and enforcers, as well as the emblems and paraphernalia of rank and formal structure. The black gangs, though they were more fluid, often had core OGs—"Old Gangsters"—with ties to the original LA organizations and who gave continuity and whatever direction the local bunch might want. The OGs tended to be in their thirties, some pushing forty, and, having proved all they needed to prove, kept a low profile because another fall could send them up for life. "Big Ron's into crack, isn't he?"

"He deals some, yeah, but what I heard, he likes to work alone. Don't like sharing, you know? Every payday weekend's Christmas for him." The officer drained his coffee cup. "Shows to go, you don't got to be smart to get rich with that crap."

Which was the real problem, and made Wager occasionally consider the benefits of drug legalization. But it wouldn't happen—too many people made too much money from keeping it illegal. "If Hocks was really working for him, was he maybe trying to push crack in someone else's territory?" Which could mean that John Erle would be just the first victim in a possible gang war. There were always squabbles and fights among members who needed to show heart, but Denver, unlike some eastern cities, hadn't yet suffered a major war over trading territory. Still, it could come. Like the flu, it was bound to arrive someday.

"I ain't heard nothing about that, but he could've been."

Blainey's head wagged. "Maybe Big Ron wants to be bigger; it does happen." He finished his sweetroll and coffee. "But if that's the case, Gabe, they gonna be some bad shit flying around, because Big Ron, he might be hungry enough to try but he's too dumb to get." He frowned and scrubbed with a paper napkin at the mustache over his heavy lips. "I sure hope that ain't what's happening. I hear anything else, I let you know. You going to talk to Big Ron?"

"Yeah."

"Want me with you?"

Wager shook his head. "Won't make any difference. If he wants me to know something, he'll tell me; if not, he won't. And there's no sense letting him guess where I got his name." Wager added, "He's not the brightest guy in the world, but he's one of the meanest I've run across."

"Ain't that the truth. You know what he told me once?"

"What's that?"

"Say he love his mama, but he love his Bloods more—they his real family."

And that, for Wager, was why there would always be gangs: because people who were too weak or too dumb to stand alone needed other people around who could make them feel strong and smart.

IT WAS MIDMORNING, and that meant Big Ron Tipton was probably still asleep; Wager pulled to the curb in front of the bungalow and crossed the tiny patch of front yard. What was left of the walk sheltered a few sprigs of grass around the broken concrete slabs, but the rest was gray dirt packed hard and bare by feet and neglect. The home was like a lot Wager had visited over the years, built in the 1930s, a main floor with another couple of rooms jammed under the hipped roof, a basement that might or might not have been finished. Probably wasn't, but could have had someone living there just the same. The roof over the front porch was held up by four pillars whose lower halves were yellow brick and whose upper halves were square wooden posts that tapered slightly and still had a few patches of brittle white paint left on them. Three wooden chairs with well-worn cushions filled the space to one side of the door; the other side was empty of everything except a scattering of cigarette butts, scraps of paper trash, an empty beer bottle on its side. Molson. Big Ron had moved up from Rolling Rock. Getting to be a real yuppie. Wager knocked and waited, knocked again.

Finally the slap of loose slippers sounded on bare boards, and a woman, almost as tall as Wager but twice as wide, appeared in the darkness behind the rusty screen. "What you want?"

"Good morning, Ms. Tipton." Wager flipped his badge case open and shut over his forefinger and tucked it back into his shirt pocket. She knew him and he knew her, but the law required an officer to identify himself. "Need to talk to Big Ron. How about waking him up for me?"

"Maybe he need his sleep more'n he need your talk, Detective Wager."

She always made his name sound like something you scraped off your shoe. But that was fine with Wager; he didn't like thinking that any of these people might believe they were friends of his. "Just trying to save your little boy a trip downtown, Ms. Tipton. Less trouble all around if we can just talk here and get it over with."

The woman made a grunting noise and disappeared, the slapping sound sharper. She received her welfare, being a poor widow and all, but her real income was a big slice of her son's dope money, which she wasn't wasting on fixing up their house any. Aside from the brand-new Coupe DeVille sitting in the rattrap of a garage behind the bungalow, they didn't spend it on much else, either. Man who cleared a couple thousand tax-free dollars on a payday weekend must have a big pile of cash stuck away somewhere.

"Mama say you want to talk to me." He had come to the door quietly in his stocking feet, wearing baggy drawers and a tank-top undershirt stretched almost transparent across his chest and stomach. There was muscle beneath the fat, and a lot of both, and he had to hunch a bit to fit under the lintel and glare out. "About what?"

"The late departed John Erle Hocks. He was doing a little work for you, right? I want to know if that's what got him scrubbed."

"The shit you talking about?" The bloodshot, wet-looking eyes staring at Wager bulged with the effort of the mind behind them. "Who say he working for me? Doing what?"

"Selling crack, Ron. It's no secret, and I don't care what you do to stay off the dole. I just want a lead on who shot John Erle."

The eyes blinked. "Wasn't me."

"That's good. I'm real glad to have your word on that, Ron." Wager smiled up into the wide, sullen face behind the screen. "Who did do it?"

"I don't know."

"But you've got some ideas. Give me some names I can talk to and I'll leave you alone."

"He say he don't know who, Detective Wager. He say it, he mean it."

"Yes, ma'am, and I believe him, too. But a smart boy like him, keeps his ears open, hears things—I bet he's got some ideas about who killed his man."

"We take care of it; that's my idea!"

"Shut up, fool!"

"Mama—"

"I tell you hush!" The woman's angry face shoved in beside one of Ron's biceps. "He say he don't know. Now that's it—you get on. You leave my boy be!"

"I wish I could, Ms. Tipton. I sure do. But Ron here's a known associate of a homicide victim, and I'm going to have to keep my eye on him in case he remembers something." And one thing Denver didn't need was a dope pusher out for revenge on another gang. Wager looked up at the glowering face and shook his head sadly. "Just have to stay on him day and night. Weekends, too. Who knows when he might remember something?"

"You stay on me, you be goddamn sorry!"

The humor left Wager's voice. "You threatening an officer?"

"Ronald Tipton you get away from here!"

"Mama—"

"Git! Now!"

The shape moved off into the gloom, its passage marked only by the creak of floorboards. Wager waited until the woman, staring hotly after her son, turned back to him. "The smart thing, Ms. Tipton, is for you to tell him that the police ought to handle it for him. We get the killer, and neither your son nor anybody he knows has to worry we'll be after him for murder. Business as usual, right?"

"He done said all he know."

"Right." Wager stuck a business card between the screen and a door brace. "But when he—or whoever—knows a little more, here's my number. Anytime." He smiled again. "After all, we are here to serve and to protect."

WAGER DIDN'T KNOW if his fishing trip with Big Ron and his mother would work, but it felt good to poke a stick into that wad of crap and it wouldn't do any harm, either. In fact, that's how most gang murders were solved—talk to enough people, promise anonymity, give plenty of opportunity for an enemy of the killer or a friend of the slain to drop a dime. And usually the tip came from a present or past member of the suspect's own gang. You started with a hint here, a possibility there, and finally a name turned up. Then you verified it and started building the case that would give the guilty bastard his fair trial. The trick this time would be to get the tip quickly, because Big Ron was dumb enough to think starting a gang war was the way to go.

Wager noted in the case journal the information linking Big Ron and the victim, as well as who Wager had talked with and what they said; when a lead did finally come in or if the case should be transferred to another detective, the journal would trace what threads ended where.

Turning to the day's memos and queries piled up on his desk, Wager found two notices of homicide suspects reputed to be in the Denver area, a lab report on a beating victim—the suspect was already in custody—which had to be filed with the case, notices of continuance and scheduling for a couple of trials requiring Wager's testimony, a request from the Houston PD for information on an unsolved homicide that seemed to have characteristics similar to one in Denver. The less important stuff included an ad for life insurance that provided a discount for public servants and gave great rates if you were a nonsmoker, in good health, and under the age of ten; a one-page police union bulletin whose headline trumpeted OFFICER SLAIN IN AURORA and had a large photograph of the victim smiling proudly in his uniform; a survey of on-the-job mileage that was due back yesterday; and a notice of the police bowling league's latest scores. Beneath it all was a telephone message: *Lab report on Hocks ready, Baird.*

Wager dialed the forensics number; Baird's familiar laconic voice answered. "The Hocks case? Just a minute, Wager."

How many other lab reports the man had piled up on his desk, Wager didn't know. But, as usual, Baird took his own sweet time. It was what made him a good technician and a lousy coworker. "You want me to send you a copy or you just want the highlights now?"

"Both."

"I should've known. One round, probably thirty-two caliber, entered the base of the skull two centimeters to the right of the spinal column, exited in the area just behind the frontal lobe. Can't be more exact than that because it took out a big chunk."

Wager visualized the path of the bullet; the pistol had been pointing upward almost parallel with the line of the boy's neck. "Sounds like an execution."

"What it looks like to me. We found dirt on his knees that looks like he was made to kneel, head on the ground, before he was shot. Dirt in the top of his left sneaker, probably scraped up when his leg jerked."

"Killed on-site?"

"Yep; no indication the body was moved. Temperature, lividity, ocular fluid, they all indicate death occurred approximately twelve to twenty-four hours before he was found. My guess is closer to twenty—only a few fly traces in the wound, and they were pretty fresh, less than a day. Probably killed the night before, say around ten to twelve, and then the flies got to him around dawn. Little buggers don't start laying eggs until daylight."

"Defensive wounds?"

"None. Hands weren't even tied. But it looks like he pissed in his pants before he was shot—the stain indicates upright position—so he knew what was coming."

Probably cried, too, but that moisture would have evaporated by the time he was found. "Anything else?"

"Pockets empty. Looks like he was searched or made to turn his pockets out before being shot. Like I say, the body wasn't moved afterward." Baird added, "I did vacuum his pockets—found traces of crack dust in both pockets."

ELIZABETH SETTLED WITH a sigh into her reclining chair and pushed it back to lift her tired and shoeless feet. "You heard about that policeman in Aurora?"

Wager nodded. "Still no suspects."

"Was it gang related?"

That was the first question almost everyone asked, as if assuming that the policeman's death was a skirmish in an ongoing battle against a vague but powerful enemy that prowled the streets for blood. The shooting had been the lead story for the evening radio and television news, and in his imagination Wager saw the scare heads of tomorrow morning's papers echoing the police union bulletin: POLICEMAN SLAIN! "No evidence, but it could be."

Another sigh as she held out her glass for a refill while

Wager poured the wine. "Roger thinks the gangs might be his campaign focus."

Roger was Roger Harmon, incumbent governor facing an election that his own polls said he would lose. They were probably right: Given the sour economy, anybody in office would lose because everybody out of office looked better. But since everyone with dreams of milking the public payroll was saying they could do better, the Republicans hadn't yet winnowed out a single candidate, and that gave Democrat Harmon some time to establish a strategy. Elizabeth had been telling Wager about some of the various aides and pundits who offered suggestions on how to salvage the election. The importance of all this for Elizabeth was not only her intense interest in politics but also the fact that the governor's party was her own. The political success of Denver's city councilpersons was less dependent on party affiliation than that of most other elective offices, but as Elizabeth had said, even when a party leader's coattails didn't offer much help, tar still splashed a long way.

"Why does he want to focus on gangs?"

"Everyone's talking about them. Television, newspapers. And now with this police slaying . . . But even if the gang threat does turn out to be Roger's key issue, I don't think he's formulated a solution. I've heard talk about everything from providing neighborhood youth centers to calling in the National Guard. But," she added, "I wouldn't be one of the first to know about his plans anyway."

"Would a gang war affect his reelection?"

"What? What's that mean?"

He told her his thoughts about Hocks and Big Ron.

"My Lord! Do you think it could really happen?"

It was only a guess, and he told her that. "I've talked to some people in the Gang Unit and Intelligence. They're getting on it for corroboration." He hoped they were getting on it. At least they had taken the information and thanked him politely.

Elizabeth dug her weekly minder out of her purse and jotted a note to call the governor's office first thing in the morning. The mayor may or may not have been briefed by the police chief about the possibility of a gang war—their weekly meetings took place on Monday mornings, and the Hocks boy had become a statistic sometime Monday night. But even if the Republican mayor knew, he wouldn't be likely to tell the Democratic governor—not if the information could be used for political purposes first. And even the possibility of such a war should be an item of concern and preparation.

But the state's political infighting was a long way from Wager's plate, if not from Elizabeth's. "What do the polls say about your reelection?"

"Marginal. But I haven't started campaigning yet. My guess is most people haven't given much thought to the city council races." Nor, both Wager and Elizabeth knew, would they until just before voting. Often just one minute before, which was why most council incumbents didn't begin their races until late. "I meant to ask, how's your cousin doing?"

Wager sighed. "I don't know—haven't had a chance to talk with Aunt Louisa for a few days. I ought to call her." Hocks's death wasn't the only reason he hadn't called her. It was also a duty he wasn't eager to remember, and when he did, something more important always came up. Perhaps because he looked for it. But now he could almost feel the woman's teary voice at his ear, and it was best over and done with. He picked up the cordless telephone resting on the end table by the couch. A woman's unfamiliar voice answered, and Wager asked for his aunt.

"Who wants to talk to her?"

"Gabe Wager. Her nephew."

"Just a minute, please."

"Gabe? You heard about Julio?"

The half-strangled sound of his aunt's voice warned him,

but the sudden numbness in his mind did not want to accept it. "No. What?"

"He's dead, Gabe. They shot him. My son—" The voice broke into a hoarse gasp. Then heavy, lurching sounds twisted at his guts.

"I'll be right over, *querida*."

5

ELIZABETH CAME WITH him. It wasn't Wager's idea,
but she insisted and Wager figured it couldn't do any harm and
might even do some good—it promised to be one of those times
when women needed other women more than they needed a man.
In fact, it was Elizabeth who reminded Wager that they should
call his mother and tell her the bad news. From there, Wager
knew, the word would go to the rest of the family and, forgetting
any differences or jealousies, they would gather around Aunt
Louisa to offer words or touches or just presence.

His mother, of course, wanted to know if Wager had caught
the murderer yet.

"No, Mom. I just heard about it. I wasn't on duty when it
happened."

"You're going to, right? I can at least tell Louisa you're
going to?"

"Whoever's on duty's working on it right now, Mom. I tell
you that."

"No, you—you should be the one, Gabe. *Es una cosa de la
familia.*"

A family thing and another detective's case—two damn

good reasons why Wager should not become involved in the homicide. But he could never explain that to his mother. And to tell the truth, he wasn't sure he could explain it to himself, either. "I'll be working on it, Mom."

He had telephoned in a request to the duty clerk before they left Elizabeth's, and by the time his Camaro nosed into a parking place along the crowded curb near his aunt's home, the reply, heralded by his call letters, came back on his radio.

"The report came in at seventeen fifty-three, Detective Wager, location West Thirty-fourth and Eliot. At eight-twelve responding officers called for a homicide detective. Detective Golding was on duty; he's at the scene now. I've advised him you would be in contact."

"Thanks." Golding would be busy at the crime scene for at least another two or three hours; Wager led Elizabeth up the narrow concrete walk to the shadowy front porch. The small dormer window that was Julio's was dark.

A man about Wager's age answered the door—Cousin Frank, Wager's mother's brother's son, and one of the kids in Wager's memory who used to play baseball with him in the streets of the Auraria barrio. When they had been kids and when there had been a barrio. He, too, had aged more than Wager thought he should.

"Hello, Gabe. Been a long time." He looked genuinely glad to see Wager.

They shook hands formally, and Wager introduced Elizabeth. "Aunt Louisa here?"

"In the living room. Cindy and Greg went down to the hospital to identify . . . ah . . . the body."

It took Wager a second to remember that Cindy was Frank's wife; Greg would be Gregorio—Aunt Louisa's husband's brother. Julio's uncle, on his father's side. "The police brought the news?"

"Yeah, I guess so." Frank led them across the small living

room to the dining room where Aunt Louisa, Wager's mother, and a couple of other women all sat at the oval table with its crocheted cloth dangling over the edges. Wager was relieved to see that his older sister's face wasn't among them; she had never forgiven him for divorcing Lorraine, and she sure as hell would not have been happy to meet Elizabeth.

One of the women whom Wager vaguely remembered as some second cousin on his grandmother's side said, "Theresa, Gabe's here."

His mother looked up. The fringed lamp over the table's center cast hard shadows in the lines of her face, and for a moment Wager glimpsed the skull beneath the flesh. Then his mother stood and beckoned him over and murmured something to Aunt Louisa, who, handkerchief jammed against her mouth, and eyes swimming with freshly started tears, stared at Wager and slowly shook her head from side to side. All he could do was hold her thin shoulders in his arm, and after a while that seemed to be enough. The circle of faces waited silently, Elizabeth joining it and dabbing a tissue at her eyes, too.

Cousin Frank, anxious for something to do, started bringing in some coffee cups and saucers, and the second cousin, the one whose name Wager hadn't yet dredged up, pushed back from the table to help him.

"Can you tell me about it, Aunt Louisa? Where Julio was going when he left the house?"

"The store." A shuddering breath. "I wanted him to go to the grocery store. Butter. Eggs. I told him he'd been around the house too long doing nothing—it was time he helped. I sent him out—" She broke down again, face hidden in her hands.

"Shhh, shhh, it's not your fault, Lou. . . ." His mother stroked the gray hair at the back of the woman's jerking head, and Wager could see a hint of anger in her eyes as she glanced at him.

But the questioning was only beginning, Wager knew. Unless Golding had a suspect already identified, sooner or later he would be here to interview Aunt Louisa, filling in the victim's last movements, probing for any information the woman might knowingly or unknowingly have. It would be easier on her if Wager did it. "Did he receive any phone calls before he left?"

"No."

"Did you notice anyone hanging around the area when he left?"

"Gabe." His mother's anger was plainer now. "You stop that. You quit acting like a cop!"

"It's all right, Theresa. He's trying to help."

And Wager was a cop. "Did Julio say anything when he left?"

"Just . . . just that he'd be back in a few—" She couldn't finish the sentence. Wager's mother said, "That's enough," and led her sister into the bedroom to lie down. A few moments later she came back. "You didn't have to do that."

"She's going to have to answer questions sooner or later, Mom."

"*¡Basta!* Let it be later, then. When she feels up to it." That topic was closed. Now her eyes glanced from Wager to Elizabeth. Wager made the introductions.

The two women studied each other; Elizabeth smiled, his mother did not.

"Elizabeth Voss. I've heard the name. Would you care for some coffee, Miss Voss?"

"Please."

"She's on the city council, Mom. That's where you heard her name."

"I know that, Gabe. Get us some milk for our coffee, will you?"

Wager could take a hint. He also took his time in the kitchen, and when he came back with the milk, the two women were seated at the table and leaning toward each other, their voices quiet as the other women watched and listened.

"I'm going over to talk to Golding," he said. "See what he can tell me." He asked Elizabeth, "You want me to take you home?"

"I'll drive her home, Gabe." His mother's voice had lost its stiffness. "Elizabeth came to pay her respects and it was very kind of her. And it'll give us a chance to talk."

Wager was sure who the subject of that talk would be; he wasn't so sure if he liked the idea. Cousin Frank's half-muffled snort didn't make him feel any better about it, either; but since childhood, Wager had heard one or another of the men of his family moan that God gave woman a tongue but the Devil gave her the will to use it. Now it was his turn to weigh the truth of that saying. On his way out, he nodded to the priest who was hurrying toward the front door.

THE CRIME SCENE was still roped off with police tape, the band of yellow plastic bobbing gently in the breeze of slowly passing traffic. Shiny black letters spelled POLICE LINE DO NOT CROSS and LINEA DE POLICIA NO CRUCES. Golding was watching the tall, thin figure of Lincoln Jones angle his camera at the chalked outline on the sidewalk. The quick glare of a strobe starkly brought out the dark red of dried blood and the stray litter of a cigarette butt, a tatter of grimy paper, a smear of spit. Then Jones circled for another angle. Archie Douglas, bent close to the ground, was carefully walking down the joint between the sidewalk and the age-darkened brick of the building wall. A scattering of graffiti marked the walls where taggers had been busy; some of it Wager could read—the WSB of the West Side Boys, an elongated rooster of the Gallos—some he couldn't. There were no doors or windows in the wall, and the nearest escape from the sidewalk was an alley about thirty yards away. Julio'd had nothing to fight back with and no chance to run anywhere.

A uniformed cop, whose arm jerked irritably as he waved the traffic past, recognized Wager. "Can you believe these god-damn people?" Then to the gaping automobiles. "Come on, you can watch it at home on TV—come on! Nothing to look at now—move along, you're blocking traffic!"

Golding, dapper in tan slacks, tweed sport coat, and suede vest, didn't seem too surprised to see Wager. "You know the victim, Gabe? One of your snitches?"

"Relative. Cousin."

"Ah. Too bad." Golding jotted the information in his note-book, just as Wager would have done. "Any ideas?"

"No. I just heard about it. What happened?"

"Drive-by. Victim exited that grocery store on the corner, was walking in this direction, and apparently a vehicle pulled up alongside him. I've got a witness at the grocery store heard three shots. Looked like at least two hit the victim, one in the body, one in the head. Victim crawled or rolled against the wall over there." He pointed to where Lincoln Jones was squatting for another photograph, this one a low-angle shot to show the background to the location. A few feet away lay a grocery sack; something inside had broken and soaked the paper dark. "No witnesses yet to the incident, no idea yet what kind of car it was." Golding shrugged. "Feels like another gang shooting to me."

"He told me he wasn't in a gang."

Golding shrugged again. "Just a theory." And they both knew that kids could lie. Especially to cops.

Wager said, "I just got through talking to his mother." He told Golding what little she had said.

The detective wrote that down in his book, too. "Saves me a trip. Thanks."

"I explained that you'd probably be by."

"Yeah? Well, see how much time I have. What you tell me, she don't know anything." Golding glanced over the protocol sheet on his clipboard to check off the steps of the investigation.

Then he looked up. "My guess, it's going to be the usual, Gabe, and pretty soon somebody's going to shoot their mouth off about doing this, and then we'll hear about it. Until then . . . no witnesses, no evidence, no case."

Wager couldn't argue against Golding's statement. He'd seen a lot of shootings that worked just that way, and in fact he had one of his own: John Erle Hocks. And just because Julio was his cousin didn't mean the boy's death would be any different from Hocks's. But a good cop wouldn't be content to sit and wait, not if he had ways of shaking things loose. "I'll do a little asking around. See if I can turn up anything."

"Hey, be my guest! I'll use any help I can get."

Wager figured that.

HIS FIRST STOP the next morning was at the yellow brick building whose chillingly familiar concrete decorations were from another era and whose very walls seemed worn by the shoulders of generations of kids. It was the high school Wager had dropped out of so long ago that he was surprised at how easily he remembered the way to the secretary's office. Maybe it was because he had been sent there so many times or because so little had changed, including the green-brown paint of the corridor. Chickenshit green they had called it then, and it looked as if the same chicken was still busy. It even took an effort not to shuffle his feet in the glare of the icy spectacles that the thin, gray-haired woman aimed at him as he stood in front of the scarred counter to be noticed.

"May I help you?"

The official politeness turned to official concern when he showed his badge and told her what he wanted.

"Yes, certainly, I'll see if he's available." She said a few words into a telephone and replaced it. "Room one-twelve, down the hall to your right."

The door said MR. KINNEY. PLEASE KNOCK. Wager did and a voice answered "Come in!" Wager did that, too. Mr. Kinney, in his thirties and prematurely bald, stood to shake hands across his desk. It was something that had never happened when, as a kid, Wager had been forced to poke his head through this same door. "I read about Julio Lucero. It's a very sad thing."

Wager agreed. "Can you tell me who he hung around with? Any names he might have mentioned?"

The lean man ran his fingertips along the fringe of dark hair above his ear and across the line of mustache above his lip. Wager wondered why men with that pattern of baldness often grew a mustache. "We haven't really seen much of him in the last three or four months—he was apparently transferring to a vocational program."

"Any names at all would be a help."

"Yes, of course." Kinney flipped open a manila folder. "There's really not much here," he said in apology. "I didn't have much contact with him—a couple of mandatory referral visits for excessive absences." He explained, "The school population's grown so much, but the staffing hasn't kept up. Anymore, the cases I know most about are crisis cases. That's all I have time for now."

"Julio wasn't a crisis case?"

"No." The man looked embarrassed. "In the past, maybe—a few years ago—excessive absence would have called for intervention. But now with addiction, pregnancy, attempted suicide, physical violence, abandonment . . . It seems cold to admit it, but we don't have much time to spend on dropouts. One of my cocounselors calls our work 'social triage.' "

Wager didn't know what "triage" meant but he heard the note of bitter surrender in Kinney's voice. "Can you tell me if Julio was tied in with a gang?" The brief newspaper story of his nephew's death had been headlined POLICE SUSPECT GANG SLAYING, and Wager figured the reporter had interviewed Golding.

"I don't have any indication of that, but it's certainly possible. No gang clothing or signs are allowed on campus, of course, but it would be naive to think that none of our students are gang members or at least affiliates." He shook his head. "But I never heard that about Julio."

"Did he have trouble with anyone? Fighting, maybe?"

Another shake of the head. "I don't have much on him at all. I'm sorry."

The counselor, by telephoning a couple of Julio's teachers who were on break, finally managed to get three names for Wager. He arranged for an interview room while he called the boys out of classes. One was absent, and the other two couldn't or wouldn't tell Wager much.

"Naw, man. I never seen Julio with no gang." Ricky Gonzales, pudgy and pockmarked, spoke with nervous rapidity. "I didn't see much of him at all, you know, since he started work out at DIA. I don't know, maybe he got connected out there, but not here, man."

Henry Solano was short and stocky, long hair brushed back in a large pompadour to give him another couple inches of height. He had very crooked teeth and a story that matched Gonzales's: "He wasn't a gang member that I know of, no sir. He didn't like school, very much. We used to talk about that a lot. But you got to get a good education. I mean, that's why I'm staying in school. I want to be an engineer, you know? And my mom and dad, they been saving up for me to go to college for a long time."

There was a lot more about Henry's future, not much about Julio's past, and nothing at all about Julio after he dropped out of school. But the question had been asked and the answers had to be listened to. When Wager finally worked his way out through the students cramming the hallways between classes, he had a curiously empty feeling—that Julio had never really existed. A student number, a name in a newspaper story, a couple people who couldn't think of anybody else the boy might have called friend. Not even a girlfriend. It was the picture of someone who had been lonely, ill directed, struggling for a purpose. Wager's own cousin, a relative. Somebody who, if Wager had bothered to think about it, might have been tossed a word or two. But he hadn't thought about it. He had thought of a lot of other things, but he hadn't thought about his own uncle's son. And now the name, like Hocks's, had turned into another statistic. But for some reason somebody else had been thinking about Julio. For some reason, somebody had waited and, to judge from the site of the murder, had planned to kill the boy. In life, Julio had been important to some unknown somebody, and now in death he, like John Erle, was finally important to Wager.

6

REPORTERS WERE LIKE flies, you shooed them away but they kept buzzing back: nagging, irritating, pompous with the self-proclaimed power of their newspaper or television station, and self-righteous because everything they said was the Truth. For Wager, the biggest blue-assed fly of them all was Gargan. When he heard the reporter's nasal voice on the telephone, he almost slammed it down. "No, Gargan. No progress yet on the Hocks shooting. We're working on it." He caught himself hiding behind an official "we" instead of using "I" and blamed Gargan for that touch of bureaucratic cowardice, too.

"You've been working on it for days, Wager. What's this I hear it was gang related? That you think it might be the start of a turf war?"

"I never said that." Not in public, anyway. But obviously Elizabeth's message had reached the governor's ears and others.

"Is there any truth to it?"

"It's an active and ongoing case, Gargan. You know what that means."

"I know you wouldn't tell me even if the goddamn case was closed!"

"Then why ask?"

"It's my job. Just like you got yours. But I do my job, Wager. And the taxpayers expect you to do yours."

"You want to accuse me in print of not doing my job, Gargan? You do that, you're going to want some damn good evidence—evidence that will stand up in court because it's going to have to!"

"You're the case officer, Wager. That makes you an official source of information. The chief of police has urged the press to use official channels in pursuing their stories. Now what am I supposed to do? Tell the chief—your boss—that the official channel refuses to cooperate?"

"Call the PIO. When I have something, I'll tell him, he'll tell you. That's official."

"That's bullshit."

"Good-bye, Gargan."

"Wait a minute—what about this: What about you being the relative of a shooting victim? The Lucero kid, Julio Lucero. He's a member of your family, right? Cousin, right?"

"What do you want to know that for, Gargan?"

"My editor thinks it's a human interest story. Put a face on crime, that kind of thing. He is your cousin, right?"

If Wager didn't tell him, the reporter would be pestering Aunt Louisa until he verified what Golding had leaked. "Yeah. He's my cousin. Was my cousin."

"So you got a personal stake in this one? Putting in overtime on it, that kind of thing?"

"I'm not on the case."

"Oh, yeah? That department policy? Officers don't investigate crimes involving their own relatives?"

"No. I don't know what the department policy is on that. I just wasn't on duty when he was shot. But I am on other cases such as Hocks. Good-bye, Gargan."

"Wait a minute, wait a minute! OK, so you're not on the case. Anyway, how do you feel about it?"

"What?"

"A homicide cop's personal reaction to murder in his own family. In his own words." He added, "And I'd like to send a photographer over for a couple pictures of you. Don't worry, he'll make you look as good as he can."

"This homicide cop's personal reaction, Gargan, is you're a goddamned fool if you can't guess how anybody would feel about it. Those are his own words and here's one more: good-bye." The receiver was still squawking when he dropped it like something filthy.

And now, in addition to a couple of homicides, he had one more thing to distract him from the vital and pressing business of answering a four-page questionnaire labeled "Participating Officers' Assessments of Interdepartmental Structural Relationships," as well as filling out a form estimating in six categories the amount of copy paper used per month—an original and three copies to be submitted.

To hell with it! Wager grabbed his radio pack and slapped his name across the location board from Office to On Duty. He might have used a little excessive force: The civilian clerk jumped at the clatter as she watched him stride out the door, shoulders stiff with his anger and the embarrassment of not being able to hide it.

THE DENVER INTERNATIONAL Airport, the largest public works project in the state in fifty years, was the site of the equally new Denver Police District Five. The police district was established and operating; the airport was supposed to be operating too, but people were taking bets on when—or, for lower odds, if—it would ever open. It wasn't the construction—

that was on schedule and only a couple months from completion; it was the fancy automated baggage-handling facility that wasn't facilitating. That, and the fact that the highly paid designers of the newest and largest airport hadn't put in any backup system for transferring luggage if the newest and largest airport's baggage-handling machine broke down. But then, technically, the machine hadn't broken down; it just couldn't get started. So now it looked like Denver, in a few months, would have a brand-new empty airport and billions of dollars in junk bonds. It was a sore issue in Elizabeth's reelection campaign; as the increasing cost of the project was passed on in taxes, there would be plenty of blame for all city officials despite the fact that the mayor and his cabinet had been the ones to make the deals, sign the contracts, and establish the parameters without bothering to inform council of all his actions.

The adjective often applied to the project was "controversial." The controversy was located on the prairie northeast of downtown, connected to the city by a thin neck of gerrymandered land whose population, coerced by various promises and threats, had voted to join the city and county of Denver. From the freshly laid Peña Boulevard, Wager could see the roof of sharp canvas peaks over the main terminal. They looked like an Arab campground and, separated from them by a quarter-mile of horizontal concourses and service buildings, the fifty-five-foot control tower erupted to dominate the level horizon. Boosters called it the biggest airport in the world, others said it was the biggest boondoggle in Denver history. Either way, it was big. The spread of equipment, men, and stacks of materials reminded Wager of one of those major amphibious landings the Marine Corps had always been so happy to do. Hanging ten or twenty feet above miles of the flat prairie around the tower was a dust cloud stirred by earthmovers and tractors, trucks and compactors, graders and scurrying vans carrying survey equipment, work crews, and busy clumps of still-mobile landscaping.

Wager found the office of D&S Contractors, one of a long row of semitruck trailers rigged with electric wires, a few small windows, a set of rough-cut wooden steps leading up to a door in the trailer's side. A brass plate bearing Mr. Tarbell's name sat on the edge of a cluttered wooden desk, and on the other side sat Mr. Tarbell. "Help you?"

Wager showed his badge and said what he wanted.

"The Lucero kid? Got shot?" Tarbell, florid and heavy jowled, made a squeaking noise through front teeth that were streaked here and there with gold trim. "Jesus. He was a nice kid, too. Hard worker."

"I heard he'd been missing a lot of work."

"Well, yeah, lately he has been sick or something. But I talked to his mother—she was worried about it so she called— and I told her I'd hold his job open. He was one of our student trainees. It's something we do for the city; give trainee jobs to deserving kids."

It wasn't exactly corporate generosity. Elizabeth had told Wager that the job program had been written into the bid requirements, along with a few other social programs such as minority hires and public art. It was the mayor's way of doing good as well as ensuring that a wide range of constituents got at least a little of the pie. Like a lot of things, the program cost had been buried in a multi-billion-dollar budget that, Elizabeth had told him disgustedly, had already run far over bid. Where it would ultimately run to, nobody seemed quite sure, but a lot of hands were stretched after it. "Can you give me the names of the people he worked with?"

"What you want them for?"

"Hasn't any other officer been out to interview them yet? A Detective Golding?"

"No. You're the first I heard about it."

Wager nodded, as much to himself as to Tarbell. "I'm talking to everybody who knew him. Maybe Julio told them something that can help me."

Tarbell thought about it for a couple of seconds, then pushed his chair back on its squealing rollers. "OK. Let's go find his crew. They're working in the north wing."

It was one of the few areas of the site that was still only partially completed. Tarbell led Wager through a vacant doorway dwarfed by a massive wall of blank concrete and into a hangarlike space of unpainted cinderblock, exposed steel beams and conduits, the shiny glitter of new ductwork. Under the roof, a raw lattice of wires and struts showed where the finished ceiling would eventually hang to hide the service piping, and from behind a temporary shield came the stuttering electric-blue glare of a welder's torch. The loud rattle of an air hammer echoed from somewhere at the other end of the long space, punctuated by the shrill beep-beep-beep of a piece of motorized equipment backing up. Here and there were stored piles of dismantled scaffolding, stacks of coiled wire, rows of gleaming elbows and Ts for the ventilation system. Pallets of cardboard boxes marked THIS SIDE UP were placed against one gray wall, and it was there they found Julio's crew, four young men busy clipping the steel bands from the boxes and piling them for salvage into fiber barrels.

Tarbell whistled sharply between his fingers to catch their attention; gesturing against the deafening clatter and echo, he pointed them outside, and Wager followed, taking a last look around the site where Julio had worked.

Tarbell told them about the boy's death. There was a murmur of "Aw, that's really shitty" and "He was a good guy, man."

"This is Detective Wager. He wants to ask you a few questions, see if you know anything that might help. You people tell him anything you know, right? And then get back to work." He glanced at Wager. "This ain't going to take too long, right? We got a pickup scheduled right after lunch."

It would take as long as it had to, but Wager only nodded. "What's your name?" he asked the youth standing closest to him.

"Roderick Hastings." Tall and muscular, somewhere in his twenties. Black. A scarred nose that looked like it had met an immovable object. Didn't like cops.

"Work with Julio long?"

"Three, four months. Since he come on the job."

"Did he ever mention any trouble he was having with anybody?"

"Naw, man. We didn't talk all that much anyway. Just shit about the job. You know."

"Did he like working here?"

Hastings's wide shoulders rose and fell. "Didn't say he did. Didn't say he didn't, neither."

"Do you know why he stopped coming to work?"

The brown eyes shifted away as he shook his head. "Just stopped coming."

"Anything you can tell me that might help me find his killer?"

Hastings gazed off toward some equipment working on one of the runways. "Naw, man. Can't think of nothing right now. Maybe I'll think of something later."

Wager handed him a business card. There was a little line for the case under the number and he wrote in "Julio Lucero." Hastings glanced at it and slipped it into his hip pocket; at least he didn't throw it away immediately. Wager called the next youth over. Tony Quaratino. Nervously bouncing on the tips of his toes while he talked, Quaratino didn't add much. "He seemed like an OK dude, you know? But we didn't talk much."

"Any idea why he stopped coming to work?"

The youth's grimy finger picked at a pimple on the side of his hairy neck as he shook his head. His other answers were negative, too, and Wager once again had the feeling that Julio had been little more than a name in these people's lives, and not a very loud one at that. He gave Quaratino a business card, too, and went to the next name.

Freddy Davenport, a spray of moles across one cheek and down his neck, and a tiny goatee. Frowning with seriousness, he shook his head. "Sorry I can't help you none. I don't know nothing about it. We just worked together's all." No, Julio had never gone out with any of the crew after work—"We goes our own ways, like"—and he hadn't seemed worried. "Just stopped coming to work's all."

"What kind of work do you do here?"

"All sorts of stuff: cleanup and salvage, like. Move stuff around, whatever."

Danny Aragon. He looked a year or two younger than the rest, and Wager noticed him letting the others go ahead. Now Aragon stood alone, fidgeting with his tattered canvas work gloves and watching Davenport slouch back into the noisy building. Before Wager had a chance to say anything, Aragon asked how it happened.

"Shot. Coming home from the grocery store."

Aragon had one of those old-looking faces you sometimes see on kids who have moved too soon into an adult world of not enough sleep and too much work. Absently, his fingers tapped at the pack of cigarettes in his shirt pocket, and Wager wondered who bought them for him. "You think it was somebody he knew?"

Wager studied the youth's worried eyes, the flat planes of his cheeks with the lines already etched into the flesh. "I think somebody had been waiting for him. Somebody who wanted him." He added, "They picked a place where Julio wouldn't have a chance, and whoever did it made sure with three bullets."

Aragon stared hard at the dirt beneath his scarred and dusty work boots.

"His mother's really broken up. He was her only son. Julio's father's dead, too. She's all alone now."

"Man . . ." He rubbed the back of his wrist against his nose, then said quickly, "I don't know what happened to him—I don't know nothing about him!"

Wager waited.

"I don't, man!"

"OK." Wager doodled something on the page of his note-book. "Where do you live, Danny?"

"Why?"

He tapped his ballpoint pen on the page. "Have to put something down. Regulations."

"Oh." Aragon told him. "That all? I can go now?"

"Julio never talked with you about anything that was bothering him?"

"No—never. Can I go now?"

Wager handed out another business card and watched the slender figure almost run toward the doorway and disappear. Then he walked back to his car, slowly.

THE END OF the week and the end of the month coincided, bringing payday and a weekend, both. Big Ron would be planning on a busy seventy-two hours of very profitable and very illegal activity. Officially off duty, Wager swung his Camaro into the one-way traffic up Marion Street and headed toward the Whittier neighborhood.

He had been right about the effect of the Aurora cop-killing on the size of newspaper headlines, and the television stations had been competing with each other to offer hard-hitting, pull-no-punches, straight-to-the-gut stories on crime scenes around the city. In fact, Julio's death had been featured on one channel, though the woman announcer who pointed down at the stained sidewalk had been careful to avoid saying he was a gang member. Just that it was one more gang-type slaying. The repeated topic on nighttime radio talk shows was the boys in the 'hood, and plenty of airtime was given anonymous voices to complain about not being understood and about how society forced them to look after themselves and their brothers any way they could.

Their message was the same: It was everybody else's fault, and society was only getting what it deserved for treating them so badly.

Official Colorado, too, shared the widespread interest in gangs; Governor Harmon's increasingly frequent press releases began to talk about plans for mandatory sentencing, longer terms for repeat offenders, and adult treatment for adult crimes regardless of the perpetrator's age. And to talk about a three-strikes-and-out bill. The latest police department statistics told Wager that total crime figures were down in the metro area—murders had dropped almost 30 percent over the last twelve months to bring a welcome easing of pressure in the homicide section—but that wasn't the message politicians were interested in during an election year. Neither the outs, who blamed crime on the incumbents, nor the ins, who pointed to the measures they were proposing, wanted to say that the streets were safer. Nor was Chief Sullivan willing to say that his department didn't need more money, more personnel, more equipment to fight more crime. Even Elizabeth, busy with the neighborhood meetings that gave her the electorate's views, said crime, youth murders, and especially gangs were the issues that kept coming up night after night. "The new statistics may say there's not as much crime, Gabe, but that's not what people perceive." She shrugged. "And besides, do you think that the crime rate we have, even if it is lower than it has been, is an acceptable one?"

"No. And I'm not saying I'll be out of a job anytime soon. I guess I'm wondering where everybody was a couple of years ago when things were a hell of a lot worse and no one seemed to care. Now there's a lot of noise, but I'm not sure it's for the right reasons."

"What's that mean?"

"It means it's an election year, Elizabeth. It's ratings time for the television stations. It's a circulation war for the newspapers."

"Aren't children still being shot? Your cousin, for example?"

He had no answer for that because it was true. But there still seemed something phony in all the attention. It was the feeling that the people who were making the most noise were somehow using the shootings, the deaths, the fears for their own profit; and when the profit had been gained, their attention would shift to some other crusade that offered a better cash flow, and not much would have changed on the street. He had tried to explain that to Elizabeth, but she kept coming up with statements like there shouldn't be any kids with guns anyway, and people should be able to walk the streets in safety, and schools should be places for academics rather than violence. Of course they should, and Wager's job was to help make that happen. But he couldn't make Elizabeth see exactly what he meant, maybe because he wasn't so certain himself. And arguing with her when he wasn't sure of his own grounds meant setting himself up. She enjoyed argument, she was good at it, and Wager—even at those times when he knew exactly what he meant—could always count on her to find some on-the-other-hand or well-what-about-this reply that left him feeling outmaneuvered. In something like this, when he couldn't yet find the words to say what he was thinking, he just felt dumb. It wasn't a feeling he liked, but he didn't blame Elizabeth for that; what he did was start going over points in his mind that he would bring up when they found time to argue about it again.

He turned off Marion onto 29th Avenue. Three or four blocks down, Fuller Park—across from Manual High School—was one of the places he might find Big Ron. Morrison Park, three blocks to the north and near Cole Middle School, was another. According to Wager's contacts in Vice and Narcotics, Big Ron wasn't supposed to be selling to the schoolkids, but the parks—put near the schools by the city planners of a less defensive time— were the favorite gathering places for various neighborhood groups. During the day it was mothers and their kids; when night came, the moms and toddlers fled, leaving the grounds to those who didn't want to be seen in daylight. By now, the sun had dropped below the mountains west of town and night was slipping into the streets in a purple-red haze of dust and exhaust fumes. Cars were starting to turn on their headlights, too, and traffic was picking up, moving not with that earlier weariness that came at the end of the workday but with the building energy of a Friday night. Payday. Money to spend, things to spend it on, and tomorrow morning for sleeping late. From one passing car came the visceral thud of stereo speakers turned full volume to drum, Wager thought, like some kind of jungle message.

Pulling to the curb near the park, he sat and studied the grassy level with its concrete benches, some still resisting vandalism, and the sodium lights just beginning to glow orange. The area was mostly open: a few trees scattered here and there, a cluster of slides and swings for small kids, few clumps of shrubbery or hedges left that could conceal rapists and muggers. On the asphalt basketball court, two youths wearing their baseball caps backwards took lazy shots at a backboard. Several figures sat on benches or strolled along the walks. A handful of boys played tag football on the worn grass at one open end. They had the high-pitched voices and excited movement that kids get when the world turns magic at dusk. But none of the shapes that Wager could see had the hulk of Big Ron. He gave it another ten and then turned up Franklin toward the narrower strip of Morrison Park. Where Humbolt formed a small cul-de-sac nipped into one side of the park sat a pair of cars. Their headlights were off, and even from this distance, Wager could tell they were real cockroaches—dented, rusty, no loss to the dealer if they were seized by a narc. Even Big Ron was smart enough not to use his Coupe DeVille for drug dealing. Wager flipped on his high beams and cruised slowly and steadily toward the cars. As he approached, puffs of exhaust showed their engines starting and they quickly pulled away, turning onto 31st. Wager took their place in the cul-de-sac and waited; five minutes later one of the cockroaches slowed at the end of the block to peer through the dusk and then speed off.

He waited some more as the darkness slowly gathered like rising water, leaving the sodium lights to show brighter and brighter cones of orange light. The kids playing football had disappeared, and now figures approached from the dark, paused and stared, moved hesitantly away; a kid on a bicycle rode slowly past and studied Wager and his car. Then he pedaled harder into the dark, his thin voice calling "Five-0, Five-0" into the waiting silence. It reminded Wager of one of the calls that haunted long summer evenings during his own childhood— "Olly olly all's in free." But this message had a less innocent purpose: "Five-0," part of the title of an old television series, was street code for a plainclothes cop. The kid was a lookout warning his dealer. Maybe even one of those who had been shouting for a pass a few minutes ago. Wager could feel the anxiety in the restless shadows at the edges of light. But no Big Ron. That was OK—Wager didn't expect to bust the man, just hassle his business a little. Let him know that his silence was going to irritate his customers and even cost him some money.

After a while, it was too dark to make out anything but the vague shapes, probably cursing Wager and sweating with eagerness, who moved back and forth hungrily on the fringe of light.

Yawning, stiff from sitting, he started his car and swung its headlights around the park to catch scattered figures in the glare. Some sat on the park benches, others stood uneasily, turning from the lights. Still no dealers selling, just increasingly anxious buyers; and no Big Ron. But he would know that Wager had been here, and why.

7

JULIO'S MASS OF Christian burial was Saturday afternoon at St. Joseph's. Wager had not been inside the redbrick
building in years, though he drove past it often enough and had
occasionally interviewed one or another of the priests about one
or another of their parishioners. He and Elizabeth found a parking place half a block down Galapago Street and walked slowly
past other parked cars toward the white stone steps that led up
to the heavy, recessed doors. As ever, Wager felt the weight of
the towering, sooty brick; the shadowed corners and yawning,
dim interior brought back the uneasy sense of intrusion and
sadness he had felt as a child when, on rare occasions, the family
had attended mass here. Before urban renewal had emptied the
Auraria barrio and its church, they had gone tq San Cajetano's.
It had been yellow and smooth outside the adobe-looking walls
and twin bell towers lifting against the sky; the windows and
eaves had been trimmed with bright red and blue paint. Inside,
its whitewashed walls had made it light, and the stained-glass
windows had brought in sunshine. But in this church, which was
narrow and tall, gloomy and cold, and hinted of the grave, the
colored glass seemed to keep the daylight out, and even the

sprays of flowers by the casket and at the altar seemed leached of color.

The organist had not yet started to play, but the shuffle of shoe leather on a gritty floor and the wet sound of tears and of purses unzipping for handkerchiefs made a constant rustle as viewers filed past the open casket and paused to whisper a prayer. Wager and Elizabeth walked up the aisle, and he genuflected to the cross that loomed over him with almost frightening nearness. Then they joined the line of people saying a last goodbye to Julio. Aunt Louisa, supported by Wager's mother and Uncle Tony, sat hunched in the front pew. The black of her dress was crisp and shiny—new mourning clothes for a new loss. His mother caught Wager's eye, and she nodded her head slightly, her glance going to Elizabeth with a somewhat warmer smile.

A waxy-looking Julio lay with his hands folded and a well-worn rosary woven between the fingers. His mother's, probably. Fell asleep using her rosary to say his prayers. Dressed like he was going to a wedding. Wager tried to think of something to say to the boy's spirit or to God or just to himself, but the only thought was that the heavy cosmetics made the corpse look awfully young. And that the mortician had done his best to hide the missing part of Julio's skull by brushing back combed and sprayed hair. But his best wasn't good enough, and through the stiff black hair you could see the white satin cushion where some of his head should have been. Wager filed past and down a side aisle to find seats in a rear pew.

Elizabeth, dabbing at her eyes with the corner of a tiny handkerchief, whispered, "He was very handsome."

"Yeah."

The sermon was brief. It was about the violence of life and the mysteries of death and God being the only refuge and peace. The half-sung words of ritual, the gray smoke rising from the swinging censer, the ceremonial movements of the altar boys and the robed priest all brought back a sharp memory of his father's funeral, and Wager was surprised to feel once again the hurt and emptiness that had made those black days of his childhood a blur of ache and yearning. As well as a repeated realization of the absoluteness of death. Squeezing his eyes shut, he stifled the burning sensation that welled up behind his nose and governed the spasm of breath that could have been a sob. It was Julio in the coffin, not Wager's father, and Wager felt some guilt and even self-contempt at the realization that he had milked self-pity out of Aunt Louisa's loss.

But despite what he had told himself, the rising note of the organ echoed from the corners of the church and from his memories as well. He tensed to keep his mind on the present, on the sounds around him, on the hard cushion under his knees. His hand, spread wide on his own thigh, pressed against the cloth of his trousers as if anchoring something. Lightly resting on the back of his hand, almost unnoticed until his eyes sought them and found focus, were Elizabeth's gloved fingers. Wager turned his hand palm up and clasped them tightly.

AT THE GRAVESIDE in Mount Olivet Cemetery, Wager had eyed the mourners, looking for faces that he didn't know. There had been several, but a question here and there of his cousins and uncles had identified them. It had been a long shot that one of Julio's murderers would show up at the funeral, but it sometimes happened. Not out of remorse but, as Wager understood it, in an effort to extend the sense of power over the victim that the murderer had enjoyed at the killing. But not this time, and on the long way back down I-70 from the cemetery, Wager and Elizabeth had been silent with their own thoughts. Finally Elizabeth sighed deeply and said, "I like your mother."

So did Wager, usually. But at first he didn't understand what that had to do with Julio. Then he realized that Elizabeth was trying to push her mind away from death.

"She likes you too." Otherwise, his mother would have behaved with an absolutely correct—and cold—formality. The "*la patrona* face," as Wager and his sisters used to call it.

"I think you are a lot alike."

He had to give that some thought. "She's older than I am."

"Idiot," she said affectionately. "I mean you both have this shell that you use to keep people at a distance until you've made up your mind about them."

Wager had seen that in his mother but not in himself. In his line of business, the people he tended to know most about kept their own distance because they were dead. And of the ones that were alive, there weren't too many he cared to know more about. "I hope she kept her distance about showing you pictures of my ex-wife."

"Lorraine? She hasn't spoken much about her."

That was a relief, and Wager hoped that his younger sister—who had taken Lorraine's side even more stridently—could manage the same self-control.

"I didn't realize how young you were when your father died."

"Sounds like you've been getting the whole family history."

"Don't get huffy—you've never told me much about your family."

"What do you want to know?"

"Nothing specific. It's just that I'm interested in you, and your family is part of you."

Whether, it seemed, he wanted it to be or not. "I haven't had too much to do with them for a long time."

"Not since your divorce from Lorraine?"

"That what my mother told you?"

"She said you felt very guilty about it." Elizabeth added quickly, "That's about all she did say, except that there was no reason to feel guilty—that Lorraine simply couldn't take being a cop's wife, and you couldn't stop being a cop."

That about summed it up, but it was the first time Wager

heard that his mother finally saw things as he did. "She said that?"

"You seem surprised."

"It's what I tried to tell them at the time: I didn't blame Lorraine, and I sure as hell don't blame myself. It just didn't work out, is all." His voice calmed. "I guess I'm surprised that all of a sudden my mother accepts it."

Elizabeth looked out the window at the spidery arcs of the Lakeside roller coaster gliding past above a fringe of trees. "I think she wants to see more of you, Gabe. You're two very proud people—and very stubborn, too. But I suspect she would be happy to forget any ill feelings that came out of your divorce."

"Well—" Wager concentrated on guiding the Camaro through a cluster of slower traffic that filled all three lanes. He wanted to say it was about time, but the truth was that not all of the estrangement was the fault of his mother and sisters. For a long time Wager had avoided them not just because they had been—and still were—friends of his ex-wife but more because they had been reminders of that bitter time. Which really wasn't their fault. "Well," he said again, "I guess I ought to visit my own mother more."

He saw that, for some reason, the comment pleased Elizabeth.

ELIZABETH DID NOT subscribe to the Sunday *Denver Post*—she preferred the *Rocky Mountain News*; their editorials tended to attack her for being too liberal—she supported sex education and free lunches in the schools, not necessarily in that order—and she said it was good to know what her opponents' latest lies were. So Wager did not see Gargan's article until he came in to work and found a clipping centered on his desk. Whoever put it there had circled the department's public relations photograph of Wager in his uniform and scrawled, *"Do You Know This Criminal?"*

There were other photographs, too, a full-page spread with a yearbook picture of Julio, Aunt Louisa standing outside the church after the funeral and unaware of the camera, a shot of their house taken from across the street. But the story Gargan wrote dealt less with Aunt Louisa and her son than with the fact that Julio was the cousin of a Denver homicide detective.

TRAGEDY TANGLES POLICE WORK! Denver's increasing violence is a daily routine for the members of its police department, but even one of its homicide detectives, dulled to the pain of others by long experience with death, could not escape feeling emotion when seventeen-year-old Julio Lucero was viciously gunned down Thursday evening as he returned home from the corner grocery store in the Barnum neighborhood by an unknown assailant or assailants who fled in an automobile after the shooting.

The youth, who attended West High School and is the son of Mrs. Louise Lucero, is also related to Detective Gabriel V. Wager of the Denver Police Department's Homicide section. Although the case is officially being pursued by Homicide Detective Maurice Golding, Wager has stated his intention to participate in the search for his relative's alleged killer or killers.

Chief Thomas Doyle, head of the Crimes Against Persons Division, which is the home of the Homicide section, has said that although the department has no established policy relating to cases being assigned to officers who happen to be relatives of victims of crime, perhaps the issue should be assessed to prevent undue exercise of police powers by any officer personally involved with a victim.

A longtime homicide detective, Wager is well known throughout the department for receiving occasional warnings for being short-tempered and occasionally overbearing in his relentless pursuit of alleged murderers, although his superiors have rated his work as acceptable. Chief Doyle stated that "The department would not want to compromise the legal standing of any case by having its investigator subject to personal bias of a nonprofessional nature."

Detective Wager refused to be interviewed by this reporter, citing family grief as his grounds for noncooperation. However, Detective Golding stated that efforts to solve the murder are proceeding apace and that progress was expected soon. The energetic and well-respected detective in his mid-thirties also stated that the police would appreciate any help from anyone who might have witnessed the death or who might have information about the killing. . . .

The article went on to describe Julio's job at DIA as well as the death of his father. Then it mentioned Wager's shock and anger at the irony of a murder in his own family, and worried about the possibility that a police officer's desire for personal revenge might distract him from solving the murders of other, less well connected citizens such as the late John Erle Hocks, a case to which Wager had been assigned. This victim's alleged killer or killers were still unapprehended, and reputedly Hocks's death was the start of a gang war. It ended with the statement that apparently no one in Denver, not even a minion of the law, was isolated from the flood of alleged gang violence that was flaming almost uncontrolled through the metropolitan area. A trailer line said, "Tomorrow: The Possibility of Open Gang Warfare Erupting in Denver."

Wager guessed that if Big Ron didn't start one soon, Gargan would have to.

HE MADE THE call from a public telephone outside a Burger King on East Colfax. As he listened to the ring, his eyes, of their own will, focused on the scar in the brick wall where a glancing bullet had chipped out a shallow hole. It was a ragged oblong about two and a half inches at the widest and maybe a quarter-inch deep—the bullet had knocked off the brick's glossy surface to leave its grainy insides open to the weather. The Anthony shooting, six—five?—years ago: a stickup gone wrong and two dead. The rough surface of the broken brick was now almost as grimy as the smoother brick around it, and you had to know what you were looking for to spot it. Wager figured it said something about his job that he remembered where so many of the city's scars were. And maybe something about his life, too. Which, by God, Gargan for all his fancy words didn't know one damn thing about.

A bored-sounding voice finally answered, and Wager asked for Fat Willy.

"Who wants him?"

Always the same question in the same slow drawl, and, even before noon on a Monday, the clack of pool balls in the background. Probably a game still in progress from last Saturday night. "Gabe."

"I see if he's around."

A minute or two later came the lurching wheeze of Willy's voice. "Heyo, my man."

"How much you pay your secretary to be a bartender, too?"

"He get a little something, just like everybody else." A half-grunted chuckle. "Everybody want something, even you, or you wouldn't be talking now."

"You got that right. I need some information."

"Right now? What's so important you got to interrupt my morning coffee?"

"It's not morning, Willy. It's almost eleven. And I'm looking for a killer."

"Shit, when ain't you? And when you gonna start catching some?"

"Don't believe everything you read in the newspapers, Willy."

"I don't read the papers, my man, just the racing form. I got my own ways of finding things out. And I bet you calling right now from a donut shop, ain't you?"

"Close—a Burger King. I want to know what you've got on Big Ron Tipton."

A few wheezing breaths as the heavy man thought. "That be about the kid got shot? The one over near the old Stapleton projects?" Fat Willy was telling Wager that he did, indeed, know what went down in his neighborhood.

"John Erle Hocks, yeah. Thirteen years old."

"Um." Breath. "That Big Ron is a mean nigger, all right. Crazy-like, you know?" Another breath and Wager could sense the man feeling his way, trying to discover what the event might mean for him without letting Wager or anyone else know what was or wasn't important about it. Life, for Fat Willy, was a poker game. "What you after with him?"

"I hear John Erle was one of his runners. I want to know if that's why he was shot."

"One of Big Ron's runners? He don't have runners. He works by hisself. Least, that's what I hear."

"I'd like to find that out for sure, Willy."

"Uh-huh. You mean maybe Big Ron trying to expand his business, like?"

"Or if someone's moving in on him."

"Either way, could be bad news all around."

"Something else; I want people to know I'm asking around about him."

"Folks hear that, they gonna be careful about doing business with him. Big Ron ain't going to like that."

"Tough shit."

"Um." In the background another clack of pool balls at the break, followed by a high-pitched laugh. "I see what I can do. And Wager—"

"Yeah?"

"Like I say, everybody get a little something, right?"

"I deal fair, Willy."

"Uh-huh."

8

HIS NEXT CALL was via his radio. The Vice and Narcotics people would be straggling into the office about now, catching up on their paperwork before meeting with the SWAT teams to set up tonight's festivities. Walt Adamo, who had been in Wager's class at the police academy and who had been miffed when Wager made detective sergeant and he didn't, had finally been promoted and found a home in V & N. It wasn't, to Wager's way of thinking, equal to the Homicide section; but then not much was.

He also knew that most good cops would think the same way: that the job they were doing—V & N or whatever—was the most important one in the department. But Wager knew absolutely that his was. Evidence: There was no statute of limitations on murder. And it didn't matter who was killed—John F. Kennedy or John Erle Hocks—it was the act itself, it was murder itself, that gave so much weight to the job he did. And maybe that was the real reason Gargan's article was still rankling so much: Running through the reporter's facts was the implication that, because a victim had been Wager's relative, he would work harder to find the killer. A personal stake that called for effort he would not give to a victim he didn't know. But Wager had never met a killer who required just ordinary effort, because murder was not just your ordinary crime—despite the familiarity corpses were gaining on television and in the newspapers. No homicide was run-of-the-mill. There were a lot of killers who were just plain dumb and careless, even more who did what they did out of an immense selfishness. There were some who were pure scum, and even a few he might have let himself feel sorry for after he had nailed them and they were convicted. But despite who they were or how they got that way, it was what they had done that counted with the law and especially with Wager; it was what they had done, not who they were or who they killed, that drove Wager to catch them.

The V & N secretary told Wager that Adamo had not yet checked in. She took his name and number and said she would leave a message he'd called, and when the phone rang Wager picked up the receiver expecting to hear Walt's voice. But it was Golding.

"Gabe—did you see that story in the paper? The one about the Lucero shooting?"

"I saw it."

"The reporter did a pretty good job, didn't he? Maybe it'll shake out some witness or something."

"Maybe."

"Yeah—well—listen. I just got a call from that reporter, Gargan's his name. He wants to know what new stuff we have on the shooting. Has he talked to you anymore about the case?"

"I don't tell Gargan much of anything, Maury. And we didn't talk about the case in the first place."

"He—ah—gave you a lot of space in that story he wrote. Like, you know, you're the officer of record or something."

"That much I told him; that I wasn't. I said he should talk to you."

"Yeah, well, he did. And he asked me all sorts of questions

about you. About how you felt getting a cousin killed and what you were doing about it. Like if you were taking it personal, you know."

"I read the story."

"Yeah, well, I hope you didn't mind my telling him. I didn't know he was going to sort of focus on that." Golding waited for Wager to tell him something more. When he didn't, Golding added, "Gargan's a nice guy; he's doing some more articles on city crime. But if he interviews you again, I don't want to come out in the newspaper looking like a idiot, you know?"

That would take some effort, but Wager kept that comment to himself. "I'm not sure what you're telling me, Maury."

"Just if Gargan does come to you for any more information on the case, we make sure our stories check out together. You know, so we don't tell him different things and sound like we don't know our ass from our elbow on this."

"We'll do it this way: It's your case, you be the one to talk with Gargan."

"You sure that's OK? After all, the Lucero kid was your cousin, and like Gargan says, that's the human interest side of the story."

"Believe me, it will not hurt my feelings."

"That's great, Gabe." There was a brief pause, then Golding offered something in return. "Hey, did I tell you about this dentist I found up in Boulder—guy who practices holistic dentistry? It's the latest in dental care. He says a person's lifestyle choices affect dental health in a big way."

"All right. I'll choose to brush my teeth after every meal."

"That's not what this guy's about. That's important, sure, but this is your whole life—that's what holistic means. The whole thing. He combines dental technology with folk medicine and orients your life to your teeth."

"To my teeth?"

"Yeah! You ever consider how central to your well-being

your teeth are? Even when you're asleep. Ever grind your teeth in your sleep?"

"Maury—"

"I'm serious, Gabe. Do you?"

"I don't know—I'm asleep."

"There, see? You don't even know whether you do or not. That's a sign you don't know how important teeth are to your entire holistic well-being."

"Golding—"

"All right, all right. It's your life. But you got to remember, Gabe, every moment you're happy is a gift to the rest of humankind. And when you're not happy, you take that gift away. You know what I mean?"

"No. Good-bye."

He seemed to be hanging up on everybody this morning. Maybe, goddamn it, if everybody would let him do his work, he would find some sweetness and light to give to the rest of humankind.

But it wasn't sweetness and light that was on his mind when Adamo from V & N finally returned his call. "You know Big Ron Tipton, Walt?"

"I wish I didn't. He kill somebody now?"

"Not that I know of." Wager explained about John Erle.

"A territorial squabble?" Adamo knew the possibility was something to worry about. "Does Intelligence have anything on it?"

"Nothing yet. You heard anything?"

"No. Maybe that's not why the kid was killed. I hope."

"I'd like some heat put on Big Ron—enough to make him want to talk to me."

"A little high-profile stuff be good enough? We're wading through shit up to our chins right now. Won't have a lot of time to develop anything much more than that for a couple of weeks."

"That'll be fine, Walt. Just enough so he knows I wasn't blowing smoke."

"You got it." Adamo was still thinking gang war. "If you hear anything more about why that kid was killed, let me know, OK?"

Wager promised he would.

"High profile" was Walt's shop talk for making an officer's presence known to a suspect. It was a form of harassment usually just inside the law: park an obvious survey vehicle on the street near his house, cruise by favorite corners and addresses where he was known to do business, have the uniformed people stop him for jaywalking or littering, that kind of thing. That arranged, Wager checked the time and then took the elevator down to the basement garage where the duty cars waited. The senior counselor at Cole Middle School had finally located some of John Erle's friends and promised to have them in his office over the noon hour for Wager to talk to.

THE BUILDING WAS a smaller version of Julio's high school: three stories of brick, this time dark red, whose sprawling wings were surrounded by asphalt that once might have been lawns. The paved areas had that grimy, tired look given by a lot of wear over a lot of years, and in the corners the wind had blown trash into little piles that gave a slightly ominous feel. It was as if the ghosts of boys who had gathered there in packs before school or during PE were still waiting to jump an isolated kid. The unyielding brick and asphalt, the sense of isolated corners and empty corridors where dark things could happen, the rows and rows of square windows that seemed to mask staring eyes, all brought back a feeling Wager had forgotten, and he could almost see himself in that first year of junior high school, a skinny runt who despite his name wasn't one of the Anglos, and despite his skin wasn't one of the Hispanics. And in the fights between the two, he had ended up battling both. That hadn't left much time for what he was supposed to be learning from books and classes, and looking back on it, he guessed that was another of the reasons he finally gave up on high school: that lost year when studies had been outweighed by survival. Not that he'd cared enough about schoolwork to try and make it up, but that's what the rigidity and grayness of this soiled building reminded him of. And the memory made the swarm of open-mouthed adolescent faces that filled the hallway seem half-familiar; among the gabbling swagger of many of the boys and the self-contained alertness of the budding girls he saw faces he almost recognized, and lives he could almost read.

He had a pretty good idea about the lives of the three kids sitting on hard chairs in the waiting room of the counselor's office, too. They eyed him when he came in, a mixture of suspicion and curiosity half-masked by a show of worldly carelessness.

"Gentlemen," Wager nodded.

Two nodded back. One just stared defensively.

Wager knocked on the door whose plastic name plate said Mr. Hoyer. A voice said "Come in," and Wager did. Hoyer was a large man whose skin glistened with its own blackness. His thick hand wrapped around Wager's in a brief, strong grip, and he nodded to one of the chairs placed in front of the desk. "The three boys are waiting for you."

"I saw them. How well did you know Hocks?"

The man's forehead wrinkled in a shrug, and Wager noted the glint of a scar leading into the short, graying hair. There were a few more tiny cuts in the puffy flesh beneath his eyes, like an ex-boxer might have. "I didn't have any official contact with him; he was doing all right in his schoolwork, I hear—one of the better students, in fact. But I did ask around, and"—another shrug—"he had some money coming from somewhere. You know, talking big, flashing it around. Lord knows he didn't get much from his mama, so it's probably like you suspected—he was working the street for somebody."

"Any names mentioned?"

"Not to me. Maybe one of those three out there know something."

"Anything you can tell me about them?"

"They hung around with John here at school; I don't know how tight they were away from here. In fact, from what I can learn John didn't have too many close friends his own age. He seemed to hang around after school with an older crowd, which would go along with what you believe."

"Any place I can talk to them privately?"

He hauled himself out of his creaking swivel chair. "Use this office—I got a class anyway." He locked his desk drawer and filing cabinet and then opened the door to point a large finger at the nearest boy. "Go on in, Londe." Hoyer turned back to Wager, speaking over Londe's head. "I hope these boys can help you, Detective Wager. John Hocks didn't deserve what happened to him—he never really had a chance."

Londe Straight was the boy's name. It wasn't the kid Wager wanted to start with, but the choice had been made; he was the one who had stared a challenge, and, slouching in the chair across from Wager's, he kept it up. "I don't have to tell you nothin'."

Straight was right; he was given a lot of protection from accessory-after-the-fact by the juvenile laws, which, Wager guessed, the lad knew as well as any judge or lawyer. It was an education but not exactly the kind the schools touted. "You know John Erle's mother, don't you? You've been over to their house, talked with Coley and Jeanette, right?"

The bony shoulders beneath the loose-fitting plaid shirt rose and fell. He wore his cloth windbreaker tied by its sleeves around his hips. An LA Raiders baseball cap, its pirate popular with several gangs, was jammed into one of the soiled pockets. Students were forbidden to wear gang colors and clothes to school, but the principal couldn't do much about what they wore coming and going home.

"You think Mrs. Hocks was very happy about burying her son?"

"Quit it!"

"How about you? Would your mother be happy about burying you?"

"Hey, man, we all got to die sometime!"

"Yeah, but how about making it later than sooner? You heard what Mr. Hoyer said: John never had a chance." Wager waited; in the building the final bell rang, and the traffic noises from the hall died away. "You think John Erle wanted to die? You think he didn't give a shit about living another day?"

"He talked the talk and he walked the walk. He knew what he was doing."

"And so that makes it all right for somebody to kill him."

"He knew what he was doing, man!"

"What was he doing, Londe?"

The boy's thick lips shut tightly.

"Did he tell you who he was working for?"

Nothing.

"Are you afraid of Big Ron?"

"I ain't afraid of nothin'!"

"You're afraid of talking to me."

"You a cop—nobody talks to cops."

Wager figured Londe was about Hocks's age—thirteen, maybe going on fourteen. Eager to be away from childhood, hungry for the big adventures talked about by kids two, three years older who were cool, man. And those kids—despite all they did talk about—knew other things that were only excited whispers that stopped when Londe showed up. "Hocks is going to be dead a long time, Londe. He's never coming back to see his mama and his sisters. Never."

The eyes blinked, and Wager saw a tiny tremor in the boy's fist.

"Only thirteen years of living—thirteen Christmases, thirteen candles on his birthday cake. And now he's dead until the end of time. That sound fair to you?"

"Man—!"

"I want to know who killed him."

His answer came in a wrenched whisper, "I don't know who done it!"

"I'm not saying you do. But I can find out a lot sooner if I know all about John Erle—what he did on the streets, who he did it for."

"Who said he was doing anything on the streets!"

Wager waited. A lot of people, including kids this age, once they started talking, had a hard time with silence.

"Who said that, man?"

Wager waited.

"How long you going to sit there like that? I got to get to class!"

"Was Hocks in the same class, Londe? How late you think he's going to be?" Wager settled more comfortably against the hard angle of his chair. "And how much do you think he'd want his killer to get away with what he did?"

"But I don't know who killed him!"

"Was Hocks selling?"

Londe sighed. " 'At's what he say. I don't know. He had him some money, though, and he was talking a lot more where that come from."

"Did he say who he was working for?"

"Not right out, no. But he was hinting around about how he just might be in with Big Ron and all. You know, talking like he know more but we was too little to tell it to. And everybody knows what Big Ron does. Even you cops." The boy's lips twisted. "He pays off the cops to let him alone, like."

"You know this or you hear this?"

A shrug. "He still in business, ain't he?"

"When did all this start to happen?"

"Couple weeks before he was killed." Londe's brown eyes looked out the window. "I reckon he didn't have much time to enjoy all that money."

"Do you know Big Ron?"

"I seen him around. Everybody seen him on account of he can't do no business without being seen. John Erle, he say you cops either getting paid off or you got to be dumber than Big Ron not to catch him."

"He thought Big Ron was dumb, did he?"

"Man, he is dumb! I mean John Erle told me he almost can't even write his own name! John Erle told me he have to read things for him because Big Ron can't do it hisself."

"Did Big Ron send John into somebody else's territory?"

Londe looked at the worn carpet and shook his head. "I don't know."

He didn't know the answers to the rest of Wager's questions either, but what he'd said confirmed what Wager had been thinking. The other two boys, although more willing to help, couldn't give any information about why Hocks would be shot. But what they did say filled out the picture of Hocks as a sharp kid with big dreams who suddenly had a lot of money to back up his bragging, enough to buy all the CDs and videos and clothes any of them wanted, and who acted both proud and secretive about where that money came from. So out of the time spent with the witnesses, Wager came away with a few more names, a clearer picture of the victim, and a rough idea of Hocks's last few days of life. And the same questions that faced him with Julio's murder: why and who?

IT WASN'T HIS case, and perhaps he should not have stopped by the DIA worksite. But Golding said he'd welcome any help he could get, so Wager decided to give him some. The decision wasn't so much the happy gift to the rest of humankind that Golding wanted but the result of a telephone call from Wager's mother. She asked about progress on Julio's murder. She said she wasn't nagging him, though neither of them believed that; she just wondered if there was any good news she could bring when she visited Louisa this evening. Wager didn't have any, so she thanked him in a tone of voice that asked him why not.

Danny Aragon drove a low-slung Chevrolet Belair old enough to belong to Wager's father. Its rusty panels were held together by strips of duct tape and hope, and the license plates were the blue-and-red Collectors Car issue. That was a way owners of older vehicles got around the emissions inspection law. But Wager figured the clunker was the kid's first automobile, because he stopped off at an auto parts store and even a car wash. Wager was mildly surprised to see the vehicle hold together under the pummeling brushes, but Aragon seemed happy, pulling to the side of the concrete apron to wipe the excess water off the patches of rust and primer paint before heading down I-25. Wager followed the gently smoking car to the Jefferson Park neighborhood and past blocks of two- and three-bedroom bungalows. Finally Aragon turned into a Taco Bell and parked. Between the bright poster-paint ads covering the plate-glass windows, Aragon spent a long time talking with one of the girls at the serving counter. Then he took a paper-wrapped meal to a vacant table. When he sat down, Wager went in after him.

"Hello, Danny." He slid into the molded plastic chair across the small table with its sprinkle of cheese and lettuce fragments.

The youth's eyes widened with surprise. "What you doing here, man!"

"I followed you." Wager glanced at the girl busily carting an armload of food to the drive-up window. She had large breasts and tightly curled blond hair that fought against a baseball cap. "Nice-looking girl. She your *chunda*?"

"Yeah." His eyes strayed to the kitchen area. "We're, you know, planning on getting married." He added, "Soon's I get a real job and she finishes school. You say you followed me?"

Wager nodded. "I got the feeling there was something you wanted to tell me about Julio, but didn't want your friends out at DIA to know about."

The young man stared at Wager for a long moment and then dipped his face under the painted advertisement for a ninety-nine-cent taco special to search the street outside.

"Nobody else tailed you," said Wager. "I've been with you since DIA."

"You were behind me all that time?"

"Checkers Auto Supply, Robowash, here."

"Man, I didn't even know you were back there!"

"You weren't looking, were you?"

"No, but—" He glanced out again.

"You worried about something?"

"No! I'm just, you know, surprised. . . ."

"What's your girl's name?"

"What? Oh—Lisa. Lisa Klovstad. Why?"

"She's a real pretty girl. You're a lucky man."

"Yeah, tell me about it." Danny smiled, a mixture of happiness and wonder, as if the life that had aged his face prematurely had for some reason decided to reward him with a miracle. "She's something fine, man."

"Good luck to the both of you."

"Thanks."

"Did you tell Julio that you and Lisa are planning to get married?"

"Yeah." He grinned at himself. "I guess I tell everybody. I guess I have a hard time believing it myself." His dark eyes gazed dreamily past Wager toward the kitchen.

"You and Julio ever double-date?"

"Us? Naw. I didn't see nothing of him off the job. On the job, yeah. We're both the same age, and all. And like I told you, we talked music." A half-embarrassed shrug. "I, like, play percussion, you know? We got a Latino band—it might go somewhere." He snorted at himself. "We got a dream, anyway, and that job out at DIA ain't going to last much longer. Mr. Tarbell says we'll be done in six weeks more."

"That sounds fine—sounds like a fine future." Wager pushed some dried-up cheese into a little pile. "Was there something you wanted to tell me about Julio?"

Danny carefully unwrapped the happy-looking waxed paper from a burrito and bit into it, finally speaking around the lump in his cheek. "You don't have to tell people about me, right? You know, if I do tell you something?" He added, remembering, "I seen that story on you in the paper. You and Julio. I didn't know he was your cousin."

"I won't tell anybody. You'll be what's called a 'confidential informant'—they're protected by law from disclosure or testifying." Or at least sometimes they were, but no sense worrying the kid with details. "Do you know who might have wanted Julio dead?"

He chewed slowly, his mind on something other than food and his fingers absently tapping the cigarette package in his shirt pocket. "I don't know about dead. I mean, there's some things that . . . well . . ." He shook his head. "But dead!"

"What things, Danny?"

"Well, nothing like I want to say for certain. But Julio, like, said something to me a couple days before he quit coming to work."

"Go on."

"He asked me was I working with Hastings and I said 'What you mean, working with him? We both work with him,' and he said 'No, I mean *working* with him.' I asked him what the hell was he talking about and he just looked kind of funny at me and said 'Nothing.' He wouldn't say no more about it, so I let it drop."

Roderick Hastings. The heavily muscled black kid who didn't like cops. The face Wager brought up to go with the name had a flat nose and wide, hairy nostrils, a narrow mustache and close-cropped hair, full pink lips. "What do you think Julio meant?"

"I don't know. I didn't even think much about it until I heard about him getting shot."

"What do you know about Hastings?"

The shoulders of the youth's frayed denim jacket rose and fell. "Seems about like everybody else. A lot of the time he's off doing stuff for Mr. Tarbell, but he puts in his time like the rest of us."

"Has Hastings worked there a long time?"

Another shrug. "He was there when I came. I think he was one of the first ones hired."

"Did he ever have any run-in with Julio?"

Danny gave that some thought. "I don't know about a run-in—not a, you know, real fight, but there was something. Hastings kind of said something now and then that made me think something had happened."

"Like what?"

"I don't know, something like, 'You know what I mean, Julio, my man' or 'Julio, you a real smart one and you want to stay that way.' "

"Was this shortly before Julio left?"

"I don't know—a week or two, maybe."

"What did Julio say?"

"Nothing. Just went on working like Hastings wasn't talking to him." He added, "Julio didn't want no trouble. He wasn't that kind."

"What did Hastings do then?"

"Laughed. Kind of a mean laugh, you know, like he was dissin' Julio."

"Hastings ever say anything to you?"

"No. Not like that. I don't want him to, either."

"Why's that?"

"You see how big that sucker is? He's had him some fights, too."

"He talk about his fights?"

"Naw, but he's got this knife cut on his shoulder and somebody flattened his nose for him. And the way he looks sometimes, you know, you can tell he don't like us, man."

"Hispanics?"

"Chicanos, yea. *La gente*." He shrugged again. "But that's his problem. I just do my work, you know?"

"Is that why he and Julio had trouble?"

Danny wagged his head slowly. "I don't think so—it wasn't that hot, like. It was more like Hastings was talking about something that only the two of them know about. Kind of secret, like."

Wager's eyes rested on the cars that pulled past the decorated window after their orders were filled at the drive-up. "Does he ever work late?"

"Overtime? Not that I know of. I asked Mr. Tarbell about me getting some overtime once. You know, save up some money for when me and Lisa get married. But he said the contract only paid for forty hours a week, so there wasn't none."

"What about the other two, how do they get along with Hastings?"

"OK, I guess. We all just show up, do our eight hours, and leave." He added, "Hastings hasn't said anything to them like he did to Julio, that I heard."

"And nothing to you?"

"No."

"You ever hear of any troubles with theft on the job? People pilfering stuff?"

He shook his head. "Nothing I heard about." He added, "I guess it could happen—there's a lot of stuff laying around out there. But there's security people after work. You know, they close the site and have patrols and all."

It was Wager's turn to nod. "Any other detective interview you about Julio?"

"No. You're the only one."

Knowing Golding, Wager wasn't surprised. He thanked the youth and told him not to say anything about their talk.

"You don't have to worry about that, man!"

THE USUAL WAD of messages and notices was waiting in his pigeonhole when he reported in the next morning. He didn't expect any urgent ones—that's what the location board and the police radio were for—but everybody who sent anything wanted you to think their crap was urgent anyway. On top of the stack was a mailer from the DA's office marked *OPEN NOW IMPORTANT*. Wager did: a single memo slid out—FROM: ADA Kolagny. TO:

Det. Sgt. G. Wager, SUBJ: Plea-bargain conference for Madeline Slusser, C.N.: 94-40-3-161. Wager stared for a long moment at the memo. What in the hell was there to bargain about? A smoking shotgun and a woman who wouldn't stop telling all and sundry how much she enjoyed shooting the son of a bitch. Shaking his head, Wager copied the time and date of the meeting into his notebook and turned to the next official envelope.

It was a photocopy of the lab report on the rounds that the coroner had dug out of Julio: .22-caliber hollow-point. The accompanying scrawl from Golding said, *"Looks like a gang bang to me, Gabe."* Golding was right—hell, even a stopped clock was right twice a day. The small caliber pointed to a cheap weapon, the kind gang-trained shooters like to use because you could throw them away without losing much money. Just good economy: Shoot a lot of people and those little things added up after a while. Wager guessed the round had come from a revolver rather than an automatic; low-cost automatics were more likely to jam than were revolvers, and everything else indicated a killer who had thought things out ahead of time. But people besides gang members knew about that, too, and Wager wasn't quite as ready as Golding to close the door on other possibilities.

He was unwrapping the string of another interoffice envelope when a civilian clerk leaned through the doorway to search across the desks and telephones and bent heads. Her eyes found him, and she hurried over, a large brown envelope in her hand.

"Chief Sullivan sent this With Dispatch for you, Sergeant Wager. It's marked Immediate Reply." She handed him the envelope with defensive quickness; a With Dispatch memo from the top floor always meant trouble, and she wasn't going to let whatever was in that envelope bite her.

He peeled open the seal. It was a single typewritten page headed SHERIFF'S OFFICE CITY AND COUNTY OF DENVER. A freshly inked Received stamp had yesterday's date and the time of delivery— 4:30 PM. The message was brief: "Notification of charges pursuant to filing: Charles Harold Neeley, DOC #636659, against Det. Sgt. Gabriel V. Wager, et alia." Another cryptic sentence cited a date and a street address, both of which Wager knew intimately: It was the time and place where Wager had shot and wounded this same Charles Harold Neeley who was now officially known by his Department of Corrections number.

"You'll have to sign this, Sergeant Wager." The clerk shoved a receipt at him. "It says you received the message."

Wager carved his initials into the form. Written notice of charges filed, date of sending notice, form for receipt of notice— Chief Sullivan was covering his ass with paper, and that hinted to Wager how much departmental help he could count on if he might need it.

"And Lieutenant Parker said he wants to see you right away." She allowed her hushed voice to show a little excitement. "I think it's about the same thing—he got a With Dispatch memo, too. He's in his office now."

Wager nodded. "Anybody looking for me, that's where I'll be."

The office of the assistant to the chief of personnel wasn't as fancy as that of the chief of police, but it was private and it had a door that could be closed. Which Parker, glancing up as Wager made a noise on its frame, gestured for Wager to do. "Sit down."

A shiny new manila folder lay among the other neat piles of paper arranged across the top of the lieutenant's desk. It had two names, black and fresh, inked on its lip: Wager's and Neeley's. Wager tossed his notice onto the waxed wood. "What is this crap?"

Parker liked to smooth his droopy mustache with his fore-finger when he was trying to figure out something to say. He was one of the eager detectives who had decided in the academy that

he was going to be chief someday and had applied to every
administrative course that opened up. It paid off for him: The
only wound he ever got was a paper cut, and six months ago he
had become the youngest lieutenant in DPD. When—following
one of the periodic organizational shuffles that administrators
called "progress"—this job had been created, he had gone for
it like a hungry trout.

"It's the Federal Civil Rights Act, Wager. Section 1983,
liability under Title 92 of the Federal Code. It's your govern-
ment at work, and its says the police can be sued in civil court
for damages if excessive force was used in an arrest, despite the
plaintiff being convicted of the crime."

"Excessive force? Neeley was coming at me with a goddamn
sawed-off shotgun!"

Parker nodded and flipped open the manila folder. "Anybody can sue anybody over anything, Wager. You know that.
Now, according to the shooting report, you were justified in
using your weapon and the shooting team cleared you of any
culpability." The finger stroked the other wing of the mustache,
and he stared hard, waiting for Wager to flinch. "But is there
anything I ought to know that didn't make it to the official file?
Anything at all?"

"It's all in the report, Lieutenant." Wager didn't blink. "Are
you named in the suit, too?"

"I wasn't here then. Chief Sullivan and Chief Doyle are
named, along with the mayor: 'Poor training and irresponsible
supervision of the named officer.' "

That figured. Some lawyer convinced Neeley to try a lawsuit.
What the hell, it wouldn't cost him anything, and he didn't have
much else to do for the next ten years. So the lawyer named the
whole chain of command, trying to uncover a deep pocket. Of
course, even if he won, Neeley wouldn't get much out of it. The
real winner—if some judge decided in Neeley's favor—would
be the lawyer, who, under the statute, would claim his fees and

expenses as part of the award. Two-hundred-plus an hour, including time spent in the toilet where he did most of his thinking. "City attorney involved?"

Parker said, "Bound to be. I don't know who's assigned yet, though. Somebody from the DA's office. You a union member or a Police Protection Association member?"

"PPA." Wager would have to arrange for an association lawyer to represent him. The plaintiff had his, the city had theirs, and Wager would need someone to look after his interests. That was what PPA insurance was all about, and he preferred that group to the union. "Let me know as soon as you find out who the city attorney is."

"Right, Sergeant. You'll be apprised at every stage of the procedure, exactly as the regulations call for." The lieutenant leaned back in his chair and stared hard at Wager. "You're absolutely certain the shooting team's report is complete?"

"I already said it was. Why?"

"The answer to that is pretty damned obvious, Sergeant. If there's something not in there, and if Neeley's lawyer brings it into court, it could cost the city—and you—a hell of a lot of money." The man started to say something else and then shrugged. "Good luck."

Wager nodded thanks.

10

THE PPA WASTED no time; Wager got a call around eleven that gave him a number and a name: Attorney Dewing. He dialed and told the male voice that answered who he was and what he wanted. A moment later Dewing came on to introduce herself. "When can we get together, Detective Wager? We better get started as soon as possible."

Wager had a few other things to do that seemed a little more important than a half-assed civil suit. Unsolved homicides, for example. "Do you know something about this that I don't?"

The line was silent for a moment. "I know these charges should be taken seriously. Unless you don't take your career seriously."

Beneath his disgust and aggravation over the issue, he felt a tiny stir of wariness at the flat, factual sound of her voice. But he said, "There's nothing in this, Counselor. It's a hot-air case by a hot-air lawyer."

"If that's the way it turns out, we'll both be happy. Now, can we meet immediately if not sooner?"

They settled for lunch, and Wager found the woman at a restaurant just off the 16th Street Mall. It was a favorite with lawyers because the highbacked cubicles lining one wall muffled conversation and provided privacy. And, it turned out, the manager ran a tab for regular customers.

"Try the halibut Provençal. It's a house specialty." The woman giving him orders was somewhere in her forties, plain looking, stocky with square shoulders, hair bobbed just as squarely across her forehead and below her ears. The haircut reminded Wager of some character in the Sunday comics that he'd followed as a kid because he liked the adventure stories and the detail in the drawings—a warrior . . . a Viking, but the guy had black hair like Wager's own . . . prince somebody . . . Prince Valiant! That was it. Went around chopping up dragons and bad guys. But it took more than a haircut to be a hero.

"I'll have the chef's salad," he said.

She looked up from the menu. "Don't like a woman telling you what to do, eh?"

"I don't like anybody telling me what to do."

"A lot of cops prefer a man to be their lawyer because they don't think a woman can cut it. If that's the way you feel, say it now."

Wager studied Dewing's gray eyes, trying to decide whether they showed anger or amusement. He decided it was a mixture of both. "As far as I'm concerned, lawyers don't have a sex. Just a won-loss record. How's yours?"

"Ha! I've won a hell of a lot more than I've lost, and I intend to keep it that way. Which is why I need your cooperation—your full cooperation—if I'm going to maintain my impressive record and continue to strike terror in the hearts of my enemies." A waitress appeared with a pad and pencil; Dewing greeted her by name and said, "The usual. And a chef's salad for my date, here." She waited until the waitress had completed the order, then focused on her client.

"I did some quick research, Detective Wager. I hear you

like to skate pretty close to the line between legal and illegal procedure."

"And whoever you telephoned probably said I made homicide detective because I'm Hispanic."

"Yes, I did hear that. However, I'll grant that you earned your rank. But suppose we get away from your ethnic defensiveness to the point I'm making: your reputation in the department for being a workaholic and for doing whatever you can to get a conviction."

"First let me make my point clear, Counselor." Wager heard in his own voice the Spanish lilt that came when he was getting angry. "The things you heard may or may not be true. I'm a cop and a damned good one, and I'm in Homicide because I do good work. As to my being the token Hispanic, it is damn well not true. As to my working hard, it is true. I like my work, Counselor; I like stepping on scum. And some of the people I work with I don't like because I don't think they earn their pay!"

She carefully buttered a piece of roll and waited until she was sure he had stopped. "I'm also told you have a quick temper. Now look how that profile could be shaped in court: a hot-tempered chili pepper of a cop who stops at nothing to get an arrest, one even resented by his fellow policemen, one who has a demonstrated record of irascibility, of challenge to higher authority, of pushing the limits of legal procedure to compensate for being a minority. In short, a bomb waiting to be touched off." Dewing raised the bread and addressed an imaginary audience: "Ladies and gentlemen of the jury, this highly unstable officer of the law grossly misused his power, resulting in violent, unnecessary, and illegal bodily injury to my poor client. And for all that we're only asking five million dollars, damages and punitive."

"The shooting report cleared me!"

"And if you believe you're going to be tried on this incident alone, you better think again. The plaintiff's lawyer is going to try your whole history as a police officer, Detective Wager. He will attempt to bring into court every report, every letter, every reprimand, every rumor that could possibly support his contention that you have shown a pattern of excessive force, that your superiors should have corrected that pattern, and that their failure to do so allowed you to maliciously wound and attempt to kill his client." The lawyer leaned against the back of the booth and swallowed half a glass of ice water. "Your superiors, of course, will be vitally interested in defending themselves against the charge of poor training and lack of supervision; they will try to show that you attended required training courses and sensitivity classes, that you consistently performed your duty to common expectations, that any unfavorable incidents in your performance of duty had been promptly pointed out to you and appropriate corrective action taken, and that any excessive force you may have used against Neeley was not their responsibility but yours. Which leaves you way out on the end of a very shaky limb. So we have to proceed, Detective Wager, as if you're facing the end of your career, and as if the facts, which you firmly believe to support your actions, are not so firm after all. For that, I need your cooperation, not just your belief that this charge is some half-assed story made up of a bunch of groundless bullshit."

Wager sipped at his own water. "You might make a good homicide detective." He meant it as a sincere compliment, and that's the way she took it.

ELIZABETH ACCEPTED THE seriousness of the charges far more quickly than Wager had, and less calmly. "It's stupid! Utterly and completely stupid! That man was trying to kill you, Gabe. You were acting in the line of duty and you had a right—even an obligation—to protect yourself and others!"

"You know it and I know it. But a jury has to know it, too."

"So you're definitely going to court? Your lawyer—what's his name? Dewey?—thinks there actually is a case against you?"

"Dewing. It's a she. And she says we'd better plan on it. She's going to ask for a dismissal on the strength of the investigation team's findings, but the judge could say no."

"It's preposterous!" In her quick anger, she had shoved aside the papers littering the coffee table and now half-absently groped for the page she had been working on. "Is your lawyer any good? I know a couple to recommend."

"I think she'll do." He spotted the paper and pushed it toward her: a scribbled draft of a position statement for the reelection campaign. It argued against offering any more tax breaks to the Denver Broncos, who were pleading poverty and patriotism in order to have the citizens of Denver donate a new stadium to them. The numbered paragraphs were marked by additions and deletions and arrows that moved sentences around. If she'd argue the other way, her campaign fund would be a lot fatter, but then she wouldn't be any different from most of the people lining up to run against her. Nor would she be honest. "Who's going to be your main opponent?"

"What? Oh—Dennis Trotter. He has the Chamber of Commerce behind him." She slapped her pencil down. "You don't seem at all worried by those charges!"

What she meant was that he didn't seem worried enough. But she was arguing more with the situation than with him, and that was something which—right now—was out of his hands. He told her that, but it took her a few more angry swings to get it out of her system. Finally, she asked, "Who is this Neeley? What kind of claim can he possibly think he has?"

"He was a suspect in a murder, a shoot-out between the Bloods and the Crips about a year ago. I wanted to arrest him and he didn't want to be arrested."

"Gangs, again!"

"Yeah. He was convicted—should have got manslaughter, but Kolagny settled for a negligent homicide plea. Kolagny would probably have given him a medal for street cleaning, but Neeley's lawyer didn't think to ask. Anyway, the scumbag's spending more time for resisting arrest and assaulting an officer than for killing a guy."

"You were the assaulted officer, of course."

Wager nodded, blinking away the sharp memory of Neeley tumbling frantically out of his car to disappear into the entrance of the old apartment building. And Wager, pausing at the door, weapon in hand, listening to the thudding feet run up the stairs and then sprinting after them. And the sudden, tense silence just over his head on the third landing. Then, at the end of a shadowed hallway, Neeley crouching in the shadowed corner like a trapped rodent hoping he was invisible. Wager could still smell the sour odor of the place: clogged drains, urine, the mustiness of caked filth. Neeley pleading, "Don't shoot, man, please don't shoot!" Then the stubbed barrel of a shotgun swung from behind his leg and Wager flung himself against a closed door for the thin protection of its sill and frantically jerked the trigger. Shoot first. Get the first round off—you don't have to hit anything, just shoot first and hope the muzzle blast and noise will screw up his aim, but the shotgun boomed, plaster and stinging fragments peppering Wager's leg as he fired again, more carefully this time, and again, before another round could be chambered into the smoking shotgun, sending Neeley doubled and grunting to the worn carpet.

He took a deep breath, coming back to the present and recognizing the various shades of blue in the painting on the wall of Elizabeth's living room, feeling his pulse slow back to normal. "He doesn't have any case at all. He's trying to build up his disability allowance for when he gets out, that's all."

"I hope that's so."

"Of course it is."

IF WAGER HAD to take a vote, he'd guess that more people sided with Elizabeth's worry than with his own confidence. His pigeonhole had three messages from Gargan—please return call—and a copy of the police union newsletter that headlined OFFICER CHARGED IN SHOOTING and named one Det. Sgt. G. V. Wager as the officer. They used the same official department photograph that Gargan had used and mentioned that since Wager wasn't a member of the union, the future of his career looked pretty grim. Even the good-morning nods from other detectives busy at their desks had a little extra, some a wag of sympathy, others a touch of satisfaction. He was doubly surprised by a note from his ex-partner, Max Axton, who was still on medical leave: *"Gabe, how many times I got to tell you—kill the bastards and then they can't sue you."* The first surprise was the note: how far and how fast the news of Neeley's charges traveled; the second surprise was the content—it sounded as if being shot finally made old Max-of-the-bleeding-heart realize there actually were people who didn't like cops. Even if, Wager smiled to himself, there didn't seem to be anyone who didn't like Max.

He shuffled quickly through the waiting paperwork, re-lieved that most of it belonged in the trash can, and then turned to his computer, keying into the central contact file. The screen told him there were at least a dozen Ronald Hastingses who had come to the official attention of some Colorado law agency and were therefore listed in the Colorado Crime Information Center. Even this early in the day, the system was overloaded with in-quiries, and Wager had to try half a dozen times before he finally got in. Then there was another wait before the machine asked for additional identifying data: Social Security number, date of birth, middle initials, description, aliases, nicknames, marks and scars. Wager pressed the number for Description and typed in AA. The racial designation used to be "Negro" but a memo had come down stating that the new term to be applied was "African-American," which—for computing purposes—was coded as AA. It was quicker to type, anyway: maybe in time the other races would be reduced to convenient letters, too: WA—White-American, HA—Hispanic-American, NA, OA; hell, some programmer would probably even break it down by sub-category: OAC—Oriental-American, Chinese; OAVN, OAJ. Which, of course, would mean Wager and a lot of others would need a slash in their initials: WA/HA. Then it would get so confusing they'd have to forget race and go back to skin color for identification, and that same programmer would be telling Wager to use BL, BR, R, Y, and W.

But visions of progress aside, the racial identification had cut his list of Hastingses by three. Then, figuring the Hastings he wanted was less than thirty something, Wager typed "DOB 1965–" and the scroll flickered again to leave only four entries. He noted their file numbers and headed for Records.

The flat-nosed face glared at Wager from the identification photograph stapled to its manila folder. Wager signed for that dossier and returned the others to the clerk. Then he settled at a worktable, ballpoint pen and notebook out, to read what the state knew about this particular citizen.

No outstanding warrants; a note that made reference to an earlier criminal life in Los Angeles, but the detailed entries only began in Colorado in 1991. Arrest for assault, no conviction. Followed by arrest for rape with charges dropped. Another arrest for assault, this time with a dangerous weapon, pled guilty and took six months' probation—Kolagny must have handled that one. No subsequent arrests. The Personal Information section listed names of known associates—only a couple of whom Wager recognized—and reputed gang affiliation: CMG Bloods. Crenshaw Mafia Gangsters Bloods, a group whose beginnings, like Hastings's, were in LA. Like them, Hastings had moved to Denver and brought with him what he had learned on those streets. Wager glanced down the rest of the file, dwelling on addresses and telephone numbers. At the time of his last arrest, our hero had been listed as "unemployed"; Wager dated and signed a note that Hastings was currently working at DIA for D & S Contractors. That was the way files were kept up to date, if enough cops took the time to do what they should do. Then he listed the names of the officers who had arrested or interviewed Hastings, checked the file back in, and headed for the basement garage.

The District Two station was on Colorado Boulevard. Just across those busy four lanes was the Park Hill Municipal Golf Course. It had one of the highest crime rates of any public facility in the city, which gave rise to a broader definition of "course hazard." As well as to some strange stories: the foursome, held up by an armed robber on the sixth hole, that had waited until they finished the eighteenth hole before reporting the crime; the fistfight over whether a ball could be moved after it had been mashed into the green by the body of a stabbed golfer. Some of the street cops had volunteered to go undercover on the course, but their suggestion hadn't gotten past the lieutenant's desk—that kind of job was more suitable for the gold shields than for the lowly patrolman, with the result that the district's lieutenants and captains could schedule time to play golf in civilian clothes and call it serving and protecting.

Wager pulled his sedan into a visitor's slot and used the side entrance to the single-story building. It led to the locker room where two or three men half-dressed in their uniforms eyed Wager with a distance that verged on hostility. For one thing, he looked like he was from a plainclothes division; for another, his was an alien face invading one of the few places a uniformed cop could find privacy from the public.

A doorless entry bent through a sharp angle and opened to

the hall that led to the duty room. Wager saw Powers sitting at a desk; the man's heavy, sloped shoulders curved forward as if to shelter the official form his pencil moved deftly across. "Hi, Andy." Powers, like Wager, had it drilled into him by some long-retired shift sergeant that police reports were to be printed legibly, not scrawled in script or dictated into a recorder like the new academy graduates were allowed to do today.

"Gabe!" He offered a hand to shake. "Let me finish this report—won't take a couple minutes. You know where the coffee is?"

Wager nodded and filled a Styrofoam cup, dropping a quarter into the coffee-fund jar with its slotted lid. He eyed the notices and bulletins stapled and tacked to the wall under a black sign that urged READ THIS. The display pattern was different but the contents were familiar. Finally, half a cup later, Powers tapped the sheets of paper into a manila folder and poured a cup of coffee for himself. "Roderick Hastings—I figured I'd be hearing more about that young man." He pulled another folder from the noisy metal drawer of a filing cabinet. "What's he into now?"

Wager shook his head. "Don't have anything definite. He's an associate of a homicide victim, and I just need a rundown on him."

A wide thumb rubbed in the gray and baggy flesh under Powers's eye as he leafed through the small stack of papers. Wager thought how this man, too, suddenly looked so much older. It wasn't so long ago that he and Wager had stood in a line of stiff new uniforms, the smell of polish and hair lotion drawn out by a hot June sun, and raised their hands to be sworn in as peace officers of the city and county of Denver. At least it didn't seem as long ago as their badge numbers said.

Powers flipped a photocopied page across the desk toward Wager. "Here's his LA rap sheet. He's another one of those jailbirds some California judge paid to leave the state, so he came here."

The Los Angeles courts, in an effort to save space in their prisons and further drain on their state tax dollars, now practiced banishment: The judge would ask a felon if he had relatives anyplace else in the country, and then provide a one-way bus ticket there. If the crook came back, he'd serve his time, plus the cost of the ticket. If not, he was no longer a burden to the California taxpayer. It was a nice way to clean up LA, but the effect was that Los Angeles had spread its criminals like a virus across the rest of the country. Somebody had even come up with a word for it: Californication.

Wager glanced down the arrest record. The information was laid out differently from a Colorado form, but Wager had seen enough from the West Coast to read it quickly. It listed a series of the usual vandalism, thefts, and assaults and finally a conviction in Anaheim for burglary. "He had relatives here?"

"A cousin, an aunt, something. Enough to get his free bus ride, anyway. I had him for assault with intent—got into a fight with one of the bartenders over at JP's Lounge and took it home with him. Came back next night and caught the guy coming out after work. Clobbered him with a sap or a set of knuckles, something. Victim never saw what hit him, spent three months in the hospital. The only witness, a hooker named LaBelle Rhone, changed her story. Figure Hastings had one of his bros talk to her."

"LaBelle? She still working?"

"You know her? Yeah, she ought to be retired by now, but what the hell—it's not like she works standing up."

"Got a current address for her?"

"Got the address she gave me, anyway." Powers thumbed through his notebook and copied a line onto a piece of paper. "Don't knock before noon."

"Is Hastings still in the CMG Bloods?"

Powers shrugged. "Haven't heard he's quit."

"You're saying he's still active?"

"I'm saying I don't know otherwise."

Wager thought about that. "Did you know he's got a job out at DIA?"

"I didn't know. Maybe he's getting religion."

Remembering the sullen glare Hastings had given him, Wager said, "Yeah." Then he said, "Any run-ins with him since the assault?"

"No. Might check with somebody in the Gang Unit, though. They might be able to tell you more."

Wager tried Powers with the names of the rest of Julio's crew, but the sergeant didn't recognize any of them. He thanked the man, and they made noises about getting together for a beer sometime, then he drove back to department headquarters. He was scarcely aware of the busy midday traffic that weaved past his slower-moving vehicle.

11

DETECTIVE FULLERTON WAS the only Gang Unit officer available. Wager stifled a groan and tried to look happy to see him as he entered the warren of cubicles and desks that made up the Gang Unit offices. He needed information and Fullerton might have it; that's what Wager would have to remind himself when the detective launched into one of his bullshit sociological theories about what he called the structures of alternative cultures.

"Heyo, Gabe—coffee?"

He nodded and waited as Fullerton rinsed somebody's mug and filled it from the bulb of steaming black liquid. There was no coffee-fund jar here; headquarters units had made their caffeine fix a line item in their budgets. They also made their coffee so bitter that no one would pay to drink it.

"I pulled the file on Hastings." Forehead wrinkling with the seriousness of the issue, he tapped the cover of a thin manila folder but held it just out of Wager's reach. "We don't have much on him so far, but he's definitely a player."

"He's active?"

"One of the OGs—Old Gangsters. You know what that means?"

"I know, Norm."

"Right. Well, my information—and this is confidential, Gabe, you understand?"

"I understand."

"My confidential information is that he's a main connection between the local CMG Bloods and the parent CMG group in LA. The local group's in the process of developing from a collectivity to a gang, and Hastings is one of the second-level organizers."

"He's some kind of leader?"

"Well, yes and no. 'Leader' is kind of an oversimplification because he's not an everyday figure in the nuclear structure. He's more of a resource and liaison figure. An adviser, you know what I mean?"

"No."

Fullerton's wiry eyebrows pulled together with the intensity of his effort to explain it. "He's a connection with the LA bunch—they're a bona fide organization, way beyond a collectivity and a lot more centralized and structured than a gang. They got a lot to teach our local people, and it's a way for the LA bunch to set up a satellite-type organizational structure. So Hastings tells the locals how to lay out a neighborhood crack distribution system, how to protect their territory, what to charge, law evasion techniques, the whole bit. Maybe even bankrolls them at first to get them set up. Then he acts as a liaison with the wholesaler, the LA organization." The frown turned into a happy smile of discovered analogy. "Think of him as a kind of a franchise consultant: helps set up a local business with advice, supply, and start-up funds."

"He makes money himself from it?"

"Oh, yeah—he gets his slice of the markup between the LA

source and the local price. That's SOP. Maybe even a piece of the local action, if the Denver people go along with it."

Wager asked the question that had troubled him on the drive over from the District Two station. "They why's he working out at DIA for minimum wage? It must be pocket change compared to what he gets off dope sales."

Fullerton frowned and thought, thought and frowned. "Cover? Maybe he needs some visible means of support. Maybe V and N has him under surveillance and he knows it. Have you checked with them?"

"Not yet."

"That's what you want to do, then, Gabe. Classic maneuver for OGs: get a low-paying job to explain their income, maintain a low profile, avoid attention so they can operate without interference." He nodded again, "You check with V and N. I bet they corroborate that."

"I'll do that, Norm. Thanks." He paused at the door, thinking of something else. "What about protection? Do the OGs provide that as part of their franchise?"

"What do you mean?"

Wager spelled it out. "Suppose another LA organization wants to set up a franchise with a different local gang, but in the same territory claimed by the CMG Bloods. A Crips gang, for instance. Would Hastings help the local Bloods hold on to their territory?"

"Oh, yeah! It varies though, with the specific situation. Sometimes it's just advice or tactics. Sometimes even negotiations—divvying up a territory, maybe. I've even heard of organizations sending in weapons and muscle if a local runs into something it can't handle by itself. You find all sorts of variables." He fished for something in one of the bottom drawers of his desk. "The Asian gangs are big on sending out enforcers all over the country. I just got a new publication on Vietnamese and Laotian gangs if you want to read it."

"Some other time, Norm. But thanks."

IT WAS LATE afternoon by the time he got back to his desk, and the ceaseless river of officialdom had washed some more papers into his pigeonhole. Among them was a memo saying that Attorney Dewing had called. Please call back. "We have bad news, Gabe."

Lawyers always used the first-person plural when they had bad news for a client. If it was good news, they took credit with the first-person singular. Wager wondered if it was a marketing technique they were taught in law school. "What is it?"

"Judge Coleman says he won't grant a motion for dismissal."

"Why not?"

"He says the plaintiff's charges are weighty enough to be heard." Dewing's voice paused for a moment. "Is there anything at all you haven't told me about the Neeley incident?"

"Why?"

"Heisterman—that's Neeley's attorney—is acting like the cat that swallowed the canary. And I know he had a meeting with Judge Coleman this morning. Even before I could ask him about the possibility of a dismissal."

"Everything's in the shooting report. I told it just like it happened."

"All right. We'll go with that, then. I'll be in touch."

Wager tried to push out of his mind the disgust he felt about having a trial. But he found that he was reading the routine paperwork twice—once when his mind was on what Dewing had said about Neeley's lawyer and then again when he forced it back to the page he held. So it was taking him a lot longer to get through the garbage, and when the telephone rang he answered it with a feeling of relief.

That was short-lived.

"This is Gargan of the *Post*, Wager. Tell me more about these charges I hear somebody brought against you. Some guy suing you for false arrest?"

"You'll find it in the court records, Gargan. Do your own work."

"So it's true? We got Wagergate now?"

"The charges are not true."

" 'The charges are not true.' " Apparently Gargan had to repeat things aloud when he wrote them down. "Want to add anything to that?"

"Just good-bye."

"I'll remind my readers that you're innocent until proven guilty. Then they can celebrate."

"All three of them will appreciate that."

This time it was Gargan who slammed down the receiver.

The next telephone call was more interesting. "You the policeman's been asking about, you know, that John Erle kid? One got shot?"

"What do you have?"

The muffled voice was silent for a moment or two, and Wager heard a bus or truck accelerate in the background. A pay phone near a traffic light. "Might have something. Ain't nothing I want to talk about on the phone, though."

"I'll meet you."

Another pause. "Corner of Dahlia and Thirtieth. Eleven tonight." The line clicked dead.

Wager wrote the date, time, and place in the little green notebook that always rode in the vest pocket of his jacket. Sometimes it was for memory's sake, other times out of habit—a clue in case some future homicide detective needed to trace out Wager's last day. Then he turned back to the waiting paperwork.

HE WAS AT home when Dewing called again. The pace of electioneering had been increasing as the days grew shorter;

one of Elizabeth's meetings for this evening was a potluck dinner at a neighborhood social club, and she wasn't certain how late it would run. So Wager had gone to his own apartment and rummaged through the refrigerator to dig out a frozen Salisbury steak. He had just settled down to unpeel the plastic sheet from the smoking wad that filled the middle compartment of the little tray when the phone rang. He had been spending so much time at Elizabeth's home that his apartment had a slightly musty, unlived-in feel to it, as if the air was seldom stirred, and even the ring of the bell seemed to echo a little. In fact, the sound surprised him—not many people had his home number. "Hello?"

"Detective Wager? That you?"

He recognized her voice. "It's me."

"I'm glad I found you. I tried that other number you gave me and left a message on the recorder, so you can disregard it when you get to it."

That would be at Elizabeth's. "OK. What's up?"

"What can you tell me about Nelda Stinney?"

"Who?"

Dewing repeated the name. "She's Heisterman's ace in the hole, Wager. Remember, I told you I thought he was acting like he had something up his sleeve? He does: a witness. Claims that Neeley tried to surrender before you shot him."

For a numb long moment, Wager stared at the wall. "That's bullshit, Counselor. Neeley said 'Don't shoot' and then brought out a sawed-off shotgun."

"The shooting report says you fired first."

"I fired when his intent was clear. Our weapons went off at just about the same time."

"Just like it says in the shooting report."

"Just like that."

"The witness says Neeley fired from the floor after he was hit. That he shot back in self-defense after he had put the gun down and raised his hands, and after you shot and wounded him."

"That's a goddamned lie! And just where was this witness standing when everything was happening?"

"She says she was looking through a crack in the door of a neighboring room. She says she heard someone shouting and opened her door to peek out. She saw Neeley set the gun down and stand up with his hands raised. Then she heard a shot. She couldn't see where it came from but she did see Neeley go down wounded. And while he was on the floor, he grabbed the shotgun and fired off a round. Then she closed the door and crawled under the bed."

"The witness is lying."

"You're sure of that."

"Whose side are you on?"

"People lie to themselves and even to God, Wager, let alone attorneys." She waited another moment. "You never heard of or saw this person?"

"No. And if she saw anything like that, why didn't she come forward earlier?"

"That's something else to ask, isn't it? For me to ask, Wager. In court. You stay the hell away from this witness, you understand? Any hint of witness tampering will get your badge faster than pissing on the mayor's shoe." She waited until he acknowledged that he'd heard her. "Do you have any witnesses that heard the shots? That can testify how closely together they were fired?"

"No. The shooting team's supposed to interview witnesses."

"Their report doesn't say anything at all about witnesses."

"Then they didn't find any. Including this Nelda whosis."

"Stinney," the attorney said. "Think they could have missed her?"

"No. Because she didn't see what she says. It didn't happen that way."

"I've looked over the shooting report, Wager. There's not a thing in it that conflicts with her story."

"Except my by-God statement about what happened!"

"That's right—nothing except your word. Against hers."

Dewing was right. The report's evidence was physical—the place where the wounded man was found, the location of the shotgun, the location of bullet holes and bloodstains. There were no corroborating statements from anyone else. Wager found himself looking at his NCO's sword hanging on the blank wall of his apartment. "She's lying, Counselor."

"All right. But it would be nice to have some proof of that. Admissible proof."

"I'll talk to Lieutenant Maholtz." He was from the Boulder PD and had headed the regional team that had been called in to assess the shooting. "Maybe he'll remember a name—somebody he didn't think was worth including in the report."

"No, you won't talk to Lieutenant Maholtz. I will. You may not like it, Detective Wager, but you have to stay out of this and let me do my job. OK?"

"Yeah. Fine."

ELIZABETH HAD SAID she would call sometime during the evening, and if they both weren't too exhausted, maybe they could meet for a drink after her last meeting. That gave Wager time to drive back over to the headquarters building and drop into the Vice and Narcotics section. It wasn't that he liked the place that much, but it was a hell of a lot better than sitting in his silent apartment and getting angry thinking about one Nelda Stinney. By this time of night, the section's officers had reported in, and most of them had been assigned to their evening's patrols and raids, the younger ones bustling out into the streets with that brisk eagerness of people looking for excitement. But Wesloski, catching up on the paperwork, was waiting for him.

"Coffee?"

Wager, learning caution this late in the day, took only half a cup. "Did you come up with anything on the local CMG Bloods and Roderick Hastings?"

"Funny you should mention that." The man was thin with a triangular face, hair brushed straight back in a high cliff above his forehead, and a bushy mustache that drooped at the corners of his mouth. From across the desk with its litter of papers on top of the glass and photographs under it, Wager could smell the odor of stale cigarette smoke from Wesloski's clothes. He was glad he wasn't spending eight hours on stakeout in a closed car with the man. "We've run across a couple of new faces lately in the crack raids—they've turned out to be CMGs. It's the first time we've contacted some of those lads."

"Fullerton says they're tied in with the LA group."

Wesloski nodded. "I got his memo on that. I think he's right for a change, and that's all we need's another goddamn pipeline to the Coast. But I haven't turned up any leads on this Hastings dude."

Wager showed him a copy of the photograph from Hastings's jacket.

Wesloski studied it and shook his head. "Never seen him around. Wouldn't forget that nose." He added, "But that don't mean anything—if he is the CMG tie to LA, he's not going to work the streets, so we'd be less likely to contact him."

"What do you have on Big Ron Tipton?"

He ran a hand up the pompadour of hair and down the back of his neck, the gesture sending out another puff of nicotine. "I've been hearing a few rumors lately about him and some goddamn gang war coming down. Walt Adamo was asking around about that yesterday, in fact. But I haven't run across anything to back it up."

Wager told him about John Erle Hocks.

"And the kid was working for Big Ron?"

"I'm pretty sure he was."

Wesloski clicked his ballpoint pen a few times. "We know Big Ron's around and dealing. But he's always worked alone and on the street, always been small-time. Sells eight balls only to the chippers he knows and doesn't go around looking for new customers. That makes him hard to catch—like a goddamn cockroach." More clicks. "This is the first I heard about him maybe expanding."

"He's a Blood," said Wager.

"Yeah—what I hear. Fuckers'll take anybody." Then Wesloski looked up at Wager, understanding. "You mean he might be tied in with this Hastings?"

"How's that strike you?"

"But he's not a CMG Blood; he's either with the Three-Niners or the NCBs—the North Carolina Bloods. And he works strictly for himself." He shook his head again. "Always has been a loner. One of these guys who learned just one way to work the street and sticks to it. Too damn bad it's a good way for him." Wesloski added, "We tried to turn one of his customers once— use him as a witness against Tipton. Somebody, and we know damn well who that somebody was, tore the poor bastard apart before he could testify. I mean wrecked him—crippled, scrambled brain, just about beat him to death. Tipton's customers know damn well what'll happen to them if they fink."

"Could the CMGs want to move in on him?"

"Always possible." Gang affiliations, both group and individual, were shifting and transient; today's Blood often became tomorrow's Crip after a squabble among the bros. "Let me talk to a few people, see what I can sniff out."

It was the best he'd be able to do for now; Wager thanked Wesloski and dropped by his now silent office. Since the Homicide section had been put on day shift as a way of saving money, the only detectives to use it at night were the duty standbys called in for a new shooting. Apparently that hadn't happened yet tonight; all the desks were empty. The Assault section, whose offices were in another corner of the Crimes Against Persons wing, were busy day and night, and from their direction came the mechanical chatter of radios and a television, mingling with the warble of telephones.

He only intended to check his home telephone recorder—Elizabeth might have called by now—but a couple of switches was all it took to access the CCIC. He typed in the name Nelda Stinney and everything else about her that he knew—which was her sex. This time was a busy time for the central files, and the computer asked him to Please Wait. He did, filling the time by calling his home phone and punching in the codes that relayed his messages. There was only one. Elizabeth's tired voice said she would be home by ten. The CCIC was still clogged with traffic; Wager turned on another computer and sent the same name to the National Crime Information Center. Their answer came back quickly: No Record. When, finally, the Colorado files gave him the same message, he headed back across town.

ELIZABETH LOOKED AS tired as she had sounded. The flesh under her eyes was puffy with weariness, and the wrinkles by her eyes and mouth that were usually faint were now dark lines. She had already taken a bath and was wrapped in a terry-cloth robe that mashed comfortably against Wager's chest. The faint perfume of soap and shampoo mingled with the fragrance of skin still warm from soaking in the hot water.

She didn't think Wager smelled as nice. "Phoo! Where have you been?"

"Talking to a chimney."

She told him about Dewing's message, and he told her about Wesloski.

"But what would your cousin have to do with something like that?"

Wager had asked himself the same question and had come up with half a dozen answers, none of them satisfactory. "Maybe Julio saw or heard something. I don't think he was actually involved in anything, not like John Erle. I don't have any evidence for it—he wasn't out on the streets, he didn't throw around any money, none of his acquaintances even hinted that he might be dealing. But someone was after him for something, and they got him."

"But so far there's no demonstrated tie between the two killings, Gabe. It's merely a post hoc argument."

Whatever the hell that was. "It's just a theory, Elizabeth. I'm not building the whole damn case on it. I'm just asking what-ifs."

"Don't get huffy. If you don't like my ideas, don't ask for them. God knows, I have other things to think about."

Wager was tired too. It had been a long day and it wasn't over yet, and he felt the familiar edginess that always grated across his nerves when a case—or this time two cases—didn't move as fast as he wanted them to. "I'm sorry. Sometimes I have a hard time letting go of work."

She smiled wryly. "So I've noticed." Then she added, "And so do I." She pulled his arm, leading him to the couch, and curled up beside him. "So let's both let go. Let's just be together for a few minutes. No talk."

Slowly, he felt the rigidity ease out of his spine and neck as the warmth of her body spread into his. Beneath his arm, she sighed deeply and nudged closer, and Wager, eyes closed, let himself drift into a comfortable darkness. "This—"

"Shhh!"

Not a word. Just silence and touch. Warmth, softness, union. But it could only last so long. "I've got to go, Elizabeth."

"Go?" Sleepily. "Where?"

"Somebody wants to tell me something about John Erle." He sighed and slowly unfolded his arm from her shoulders. "I'm supposed to be there in twenty minutes."

"Oh for goodness' sake—there is truly no rest for the weary." She blinked and yawned and rubbed her eyes. "I was almost asleep."

He stood, pulling his coat on over his holster and pistol. "Best thing for you. You go on and get some rest—I'll call you in the morning."

"I'll be in the Transportation Committee meeting until noon."

"Call you then—maybe we can have lunch together."

HE COULD STILL smell her perfume and feel the softness of her lips and tongue against his as he guided the Camaro toward the north side of the city. Thirtieth Avenue ran parallel and a block south of Martin Luther King Boulevard, and he made good time on the almost empty street, even managing to catch a green at Colorado Boulevard's long light. Then he began reading the street signs for Dahlia. Double alphabet in this part of town: Bellaire, Birch, Clermont, Cherry, Dexter . . . He turned right at Dahlia, slowing to a cruise through the quiet intersection a block down the street. The lingering warm sensation of being with Elizabeth was gone now, replaced by a close study of the neighborhood. The orange sodium light up in the leafy branches showed all four corners empty. Silent homes filled three, and on the southwest corner loomed the dark box of Stedman Elementary School, a large square of freshly painted but shadowy walls, fenced playground, closed windows giving watery reflections of the slow passage of his headlights. Circling the block, he crossed the intersection from west to east; still nothing. His watch said 10:23. Wager circled the area on the surrounding streets, checking parked cars and peering into the shadows of nearby shrubbery and hedges; then he came back to the intersection from the south and coasted to the curb to stop where the streetlight shone brightest.

Two minutes. Five minutes past time. Wager opened his window to the cold night air and slouched down in the seat, listening for the noise of an approaching car. No headlights shone in his rearview mirrors; no movement in the streets he could see through the windshield. Eight, nine minutes past.

Later, he would not be able to say what warned him. Maybe he had glimpsed a reflected movement in the windshield or one of the rearview mirrors, maybe he had heard the click of a bolt going back, maybe his guardian angel had been on duty. Probably it was just luck, but however it was explained, Wager knew someone had come swiftly from somewhere out of the dark to the rider's side of the car, and an instant before that window shattered in the stuttering roar and glare of a weapon, he had flung himself down below the seat, thumb already flipping open the holster strap. A string of explosions flashed heat across his hand and he could feel the sting of glass and burning powder in the flesh of his cheek. But he couldn't hear anything, not even the pop of his own weapon spearing orange sparks toward the flaring muzzle of an automatic weapon. His finger jerked as rapidly as it could but it was acting on its own—his mind, like his ears, was numb and his only thought, if it could be called that, was to kill.

Then the splattering glare was gone, and Wager, blinking purple blossoms of flame, tried to see the running figure, tried to yank open his door and run after the disappearing shape, tried to move but was tangled in the well beneath the steering wheel, his legs twisted among the pedals and ragged beads of glass flung through the car. Something was stinging somewhere in his right shoulder, and somehow he'd banged his head against a knob on the dash. But he wasn't hit. He didn't think he had been hit. Christ alone knew how many bullets had been sprayed through the car, but Wager's arms and legs worked, and he slowly untwisted himself and crawled up onto the seat. There was only that slight sting in the top of his shoulder for some reason, a sharp tingling that began to increase in heat; his hand dug inside his shirt and met the slick, sticky feel of something wet, and then he was aware that the flesh of his armpit was gummy with blood.

12

"AND IT DIDN'T cross your mind that it might be a setup?"

It was hard to tell if the chief was glad or disgusted that Wager was alive. In the face of No Smoking signs and pictures of crossed-out cigarettes, Doyle, wearing rumpled civilian clothes, chewed on an unlit cigar. The motion made his lower teeth even more prominent and bulldoglike, but Wager knew from past experience that the glimmer of teeth was not a smile.

"You were off duty, right?"

"But I was on a case."

What they were really talking about was who would pay for repairing Wager's car, the city or his own insurance. Wager had a damn good idea that it would be his rates going up to cover some very expensive bodywork. Landrum of the forensics team said he counted twelve bullet holes in the door and thirty-three in the roof. The shell casings they found were from an MP-5, he said, which, on fully automatic, could spew 600 rounds a minute. "Not your usual ambush weapon, Gabe. Somebody really wanted you. Too bad they didn't know how to use the damn thing."

"How are you feeling?"

That was Doyle again. "Hard to say. Not bad." In fact, his left arm felt about as sore from the tetanus shot as his right arm from the bullet. But the Valium or whatever was dripping into his wrist from the dangling bottle was starting to work; Wager could feel the soft untwisting of muscles and nerves, a sense of peace that made it hard to care what Doyle was saying. A single round had cut into the top of his trapezius muscle, half an inch from his neck and an inch and a quarter from his carotid artery. Life, as they said, was a game of inches. It must have been one of the first bullets—the rest had gone high as the muzzle of the weapon walked up. Landrum was right, the shooter had not known how to control an automatic weapon and apparently held it clip down like he saw in the movies.

"We couldn't find any blood outside the car. Landrum figures you missed the assailant."

"Too bad."

"Not too bad. All's we need's another goddamn lawsuit like Neeley's." The cigar worked its way across Doyle's lower lip to the other corner of his mouth. "Well, you feel up to making a statement? Stenographer's outside."

"Sure."

"All right. As of now, you're on medical leave until the doc clears you for duty. But I'll want a full report on my desk in twenty-four hours." He paused and looked down at Wager, who, sleepier now, wondered if the man was going to pat him on the head or wish him good health or say he was sorry Wager got hit. Instead he only muttered "Damn fool!" and slammed the door behind him. A minute later, the stenographer, armed with a portable recorder, settled into the chair beside his bed.

"This won't take long," she smiled. "Can you just tell me where you were and exactly what happened?"

FIRST CAME HIS breakfast and then came Elizabeth, her eyes wide with anxiety. "Gabe—are you all right?"

"I thought you had a committee meeting."

"I'll get there. What on earth happened? How badly are you hurt?"

"Not bad." He told her about the ambush. "I'm all right. Cleaned, patched, and"—he winced as his shoulder moved—"sore. But nothing serious." Then he added what he just realized. "I'm glad to see you, Liz."

"Well, I don't know if I'm glad to see you in here." She dropped into the chair beside the bed and poured herself a paper cup of water from the plastic thermos, drinking it quickly. "Do you need anything? Is there something I can do?"

He started to shake his head, but the soreness stopped him. "No—I'll be out this morning. Doyle wants me to take some sick leave, but . . ."

She finished it for him. "But you want to get the person who shot you."

"If they'll do it to a cop, they'll do it to anybody." The saying was police folk wisdom and might or might not have had some truth to it. Besides, there was someone he was anxious to talk to.

"When you left last night, I didn't know you were going someplace dangerous." There was a faint note of injured feelings. "You didn't tell me it could turn into something like this."

"Hey, I didn't know either! Or I wouldn't have been there." Or at least he wouldn't have been there alone and with just a pistol. Anyplace a cop went could turn dangerous. If you knew about it ahead of time, you planned and went prepared; if not, you tried to stay alert. And, as Doyle's disgust had emphasized, you didn't stick your neck out if you didn't have backup. Not just because it might cost the city and county of Denver higher insurance premiums, but mostly because the perpetrator had a better chance of escaping.

"I suppose," said Elizabeth, the note of hurt replaced by one of touchiness, "that patronizing phrase means that I should have known how dangerous your work is."

"Whoa, I didn't say that—"

"But of course a strong silent macho type like you, you're going to protect the helpless little female by not telling her. Because you don't think she's capable of comprehending what you do for a living, is that it?"

"Damn it, Elizabeth, that's not what I meant—ouch!"

Sitting up quickly had twisted the soreness, and she winced with him. "Lie back." Then, "What I'm saying, Gabe, is that I want you to be open with me. I don't want to be protected or sheltered or any of those other clichés that men use to define women. I'm an adult, I've looked after myself for a long time, and I've even raised a son. I don't need to be sheltered from the world."

"The next time I know somebody's going to shoot me, Elizabeth, I'll tell you."

"Please do!"

Something had been aired but not resolved, and Wager still wasn't sure what it was. These days, women seemed to go around looking for insult, eager to jump on the slightest phrase or careless word as if every man was in some way guilty of attacking them. But this brief spat hadn't been the same as fighting with Lorraine; his ex-wife's anger had come from hatred and jealousy—she had been jealous of his job, of the time it took away from her, of the attention and dedication it required from Wager. And her hatred of his work and what it cost had transferred to him. And, he now realized, he had returned that hatred; he had been jealous of his job, too—and perhaps still was. But Elizabeth wasn't Lorraine; she didn't need to make him less a cop or try to come between him and his job—she had one of her own. Wager understood now that he had not wished to share with

Lorraine because he felt threatened by her constant worry and the way she had used that worry to suck at him. Elizabeth wasn't a vampire. She was concerned, but she also had her own role and strength separate from Wager's. And the reason for her anger was different, too; there was a substance to it that Wager sensed more than understood: He had carelessly indicated that he took her for granted and that pissed her off. Just as it would have if she had said it to him, and he valued that sense of self-worth and pride in her. "I'm sorry."

"Does it hurt very much?"

This time he remembered not to shake his head. "No . . . well, yeah, sometimes. It'll be worse tomorrow and then start getting better." He asked, "How'd you find out about this?"

"Someone from the Homicide office called—a clerk, I think."

Again, the soreness stopped Wager from nodding. As required by regulations, he'd left Elizabeth's number as one of the places he could be reached when he was off duty; he'd have to thank Esther for looking after him.

"Have you called your mother yet?" asked Elizabeth.

"No. Why?"

She was genuinely surprised. "Because you've just been shot, Gabe!"

And so was he. "But I'm not hurt that bad and I'm not going to be here that long. There's nothing to get all upset about."

"You're going to let your mother learn about it from the newspapers . . .? Don't you think that's just a little bit callous? Don't you think she might be just a little upset to find out about it that way?"

It really hadn't crossed his mind that his mother would be worried about him, because he wasn't worried about himself. But once again Elizabeth was right—she was right a lot of times when it came to dealing with people. "OK, I'll call."

She handed him the telephone. "Now."

IT WAS AFTER ten by the time the doctor had examined Wager and told him how to care for the wound and when to report back for a follow-up. Then all the paperwork had to be filled out and signed. The duty stenographer had called twice to clarify unintelligible passages on the tape. They had been made toward the end of the interview last night when Wager was slipping into drugged sleep. One was in answer to a question about the description of the assailant: No, Wager could not describe him. The gunflashes had blinded him and the chaos of the moment disoriented him. The second question had to do with where he thought his rounds had gone. He vaguely remembered that his answer last night had been "Who in the shit knows?" but by then his voice was so slurred that the words were indistinct. This morning, he simply said, "Unobserved."

Attorney Dewing had called, too. She said it was because she heard he'd been shot, but Wager guessed it was to find out if the Neeley case, along with her client, was still alive. "I talked with Lieutenant Maholtz earlier this morning. He says he never heard of Nelda Stinney and that they didn't find any witnesses to the Neeley shoot-out at all."

"So how did Neeley's lawyer find her?"

"Apparently, Heisterman went over to the apartment house and knocked on the doors. Stinney answered."

"She didn't see what she says she saw!"

"OK—I know. And we can attack it as a memory recalled a year after the incident and under suggestive questioning. But Stinney also said that she was so afraid after the shooting that she didn't answer the door when someone knocked. Unfortunately, Maholtz said that he thought the shooting looked open and shut—self-defense against an armed attacker. As a result, they only canvassed the area for witnesses one time and that was the night of the incident. So it is possible he missed her."

"You're saying Maholtz did a half-assed job so now my career's on the line."

"It is if Stinney's story holds up."

"She's lying."

"Why would she?"

It was a good question, and Wager didn't know. But by God somebody should find out. Nor did he know why any cop from Boulder, of all places, would be put in charge of something as important as a shooting team—especially the team investigating Wager's shooting. Bunch of feel-good community workers up there who wouldn't know real crime if it bit them in the ass! "Heisterman was the name of Neeley's lawyer at his original trial— I remembered that this morning. Has to be the same Heisterman."

Dewing agreed. "Be hard to find two with that name. But that means he practices both criminal and civil law."

"So?"

"Nothing—it's just unusual, that's all. Especially if he's established. Specialty practice is where most of the money is nowadays."

"Money's what he's going for wherever it is—a contingency fee out of the settlement." Wager added, "What the hell's he got to lose except a little time?"

"A lot, if he knows his witness is perjured, Detective Wager. A hell of a lot." Then she admitted, "But he could always say he didn't know."

Wager caught a cab home and was on the telephone as soon as he got there. His first call was to his insurance company to report the damage and to get authorization to rent a replacement car, and his second call was to the rental company they recommended. The third was to Walt Adamo's home. His wife hesitantly said she didn't know if he was awake yet, but a few seconds later a rusty voice croaked, "Hello?"

"It's Gabe. Did you have anybody sitting on Big Ron Tipton last night?"

"You OK, Gabe? I heard you went down last night—you OK?"

"Yeah, fine. Nothing serious. Big Ron—was he under surveillance last night between ten and twelve?"

The line was silent while Adamo thought. "I asked Schuyler to swing by Big Ron's house a couple times. I don't know if he saw him or not."

Schuyler was one of the patrolmen who had been in District Two for almost fifteen years. He was also one of the officers who had responded to Wager's call for help last night. "Nobody else? I saw Schuyler last night—he was coming off some big traffic accident. Bitching about spending half his tour directing traffic."

"Nobody. Like I told you, Gabe, we don't have enough manpower to take on too much extra right now. You just wanted some high-profile stuff anyway, right? I mean that's all I can come up with for a while."

"No problem, Walt. Just wanted to check out the possibility." And that meant Big Ron could have been the one behind the MP-5. Tired of Wager hassling him, quick-tempered and mean, and dumb enough to prove to the rest of the 'hood that nobody dissed the Big Ron.

"Say, uh, Gabe." Adamo's voice dropped to a private murmur. "If you need some help with Big Ron—you know, the shooting and all, you just let me know, OK?"

"If I find out it was him, I may do that, Walt. Thanks."

"You got it—anytime."

Wager shrugged carefully into his jacket, surprised once again at how many times a trapezius muscle was used. He might be on medical leave, but all that meant was he could postpone the routine paperwork for a couple of days.

THE WOMAN WHO answered the door was just as happy to see Wager as she had been the last time. "What you want now?" The odor of something frying drifted out with her.

"Need to talk to your little boy, Mrs. Tipton."

"He ain't here."

Wager gingerly tucked his badge case away in his vest pocket. "I'm going to put out a warrant on him if I can't find him in the next hour, Mrs. Tipton. He's wanted for questioning about a shooting last night."

"For a what?"

"Do you know where I can find him?"

"He didn't shoot nobody! How come you always coming round saying he shot somebody? He didn't shoot nobody!"

"Do you know where he is or not?"

Her lips clapped shut, and she stared hotly at him. "Jus' a minute." The heels of her slippers smacked their way back into the odor, and Wager heard her voice mumble a one-sided conversation. Then the smacking came back. "He over at a friend's house. He say he meet you at Curtis Park. You know where that firehouse is at? He say he meet you across from there."

"Thank you, ma'am."

It was midday, overcast, and hot, and the tired patches of grass and sand in the park were almost empty of people. Wager pulled his rental into the no-parking stretch of curb near the firehouse and waited. Fresh graffiti had been sprayed over fresh paint on the wall of the station, a conflict of red and blue scrawls and symbols that had been crossed out, superimposed, added, in the continuing struggle between taggers. About chest high, a large pair of black circles with dots in the center mimicked a pair of staring eyes, and beneath, where the nose should be, were the spread wings of what might have been an eagle, but it looked like a buzzard or maybe an odd mustache. Probably the Aguilas, and the eyes meant that it was their territory and they were watching it. But it wouldn't be long before some other gang, new or established, drew an X through it and sprayed their own markings. In a way, it was like dogs and fireplugs.

Wager spotted the large figure in his rearview mirror. Big Ron was wearing stained dungarees cut off roughly at midcalf, bright red sneakers and matching baseball cap, a shirt of some kind of tan color that sagged loosely to hide his belt and pockets and any weapons or contraband he might tote. This time Wager got out of the car and rested his hand on his weapon. The waddling figure neither paused nor hurried but walked steadily toward Wager until he stopped a couple of arms' lengths away. His shadow was a wide circle of black at his feet.

"Mama says you want to talk."

"Tell me where you were last night, Ron. At ten minutes after eleven. And don't try to jerk me around."

The eyes slowly blinked three or four times before he asked, "What for?"

"Because you need an alibi."

"Alibi. What for I need a alibi?"

"Because I think you were shooting at me." Wager added, "And it better be a goddamned good alibi."

The wide face clouded and the eyes blinked again. "I wasn't shooting at nobody, last night."

He made it sound like an exception to his usual behavior. Wager opened the car's rear door. "You want to volunteer to ride with me down to headquarters, or you want me to send a patrol car after you?"

"You arresting me? What for?"

"I'm inviting you to answer some questions. You threatened me a few weeks ago, remember? And last night I was shot at. Are you coming with me or do you want me to call a patrol car?" He tapped the radio riding on his hip. The gesture also revealed the pistol stuck in his belt. Wager hadn't placed it there for intimidation; a strap on his shoulder holster rubbed across his wound. But the bulging, dark eyes rested on the pistol thoughtfully for a long moment before the pumpkin-sized head nodded.

It wasn't technically an arrest yet, or at least Wager could claim that the man cooperated with his request to come to the station for questioning. So no official paperwork was needed. Big Ron's flesh spilled over the sides of the heavy chair in the interview room, and his torso dwarfed the metal table bolted to the floor. Wager, his back against the silver of the large two-way mirror that shielded the viewing room on the other side, watched Doty unpack items from his kit. The lab man had told Wager that the results would be chancy—you weren't supposed to test flesh for gunshot residue more than six hours after a shooting. For one thing, the trace evidence could wear off in that time; for another, the suspect might have washed his hands. Wager said he didn't think Big Ron ever washed anything, and that it was worth a chance.

Big Ron had denied that he was anywhere near the east side of the city last night and that at the time Wager was being shot at, he, Big Ron, had been over with some of his bros at an apartment on Welton Street having a party. He could prove it, too, if Wager would just call over there and ask anybody, and then he could cut out all this cheap shit of hassling somebody who hadn't done nothing to nobody. Following people around. Come banging on peopleses' doors all hours. Say people been shooting people they don't even know. Making people afraid to even be seen talking to him.

"If you didn't fire a weapon last night, then you won't mind having your hands tested for residue, right?"

"My what for what?"

"Your hands. Run a test on them to find out if you've fired a weapon recently. You've got nothing to be afraid of, right, Ron?" He added, "It won't hurt."

He had sat, eyes blinking as thoughts worked their way across his mind and Wager waited. Finally, "You don't find nothing, you quit fuckin' around with me, right?"

"Sure," Wager lied.

"Then let's do it."

Doty sprinkled a little talcum on his own hands and slipped into a pair of disposable rubber gloves. Then he unscrewed the cap of a brown bottle labeled Dilute Nitric Acid (5%) and stirred a couple of cotton swabs in the contents. He stroked the swabs along the back of Tipton's broad hand, running out of moisture and having to wet a third swab. "Damn big hands." Then placed the swabs in a plastic Baggie, and, with a marking pencil, labeled, initialed, and dated the bag. Then, following the same careful procedure of identification, he used new swabs to stroke the palm of that hand and the back and palm of the left hand. Next, he dipped another swab into the nitric acid solution and placed it in its own Baggie labeled Control Swab. In another Baggie, resting in the metal tool box that served as his portable office, was one of the shell casings that Landrum had picked up early this morning at the shooting scene. It, too, had a swab. "OK, Gabe. Be about a half hour."

It was. Wager picked up the telephone as he watched Big Ron. The man loomed at the side of Wager's desk and gazed around the Homicide office with open curiosity, studying the Wanted and Alert posters, watching the other detectives busy at their telephones, listening to the traffic on Wager's radio sitting in its charger on his desk.

"No traces, Wager. Twelve hours is a long time."

"An MP-five kicks out a lot of powder."

"Yeah, that's true. And if he didn't wash his hands there might have been some residue from all those rounds, even after twelve hours. In fact, if he hasn't washed his hands I'd say the odds are against his having fired that weapon."

And, as Wager had said, he didn't think Big Ron washed very often at all.

"Too bad you don't have his clothes. Residue stays in clothes a lot longer."

"Yeah—thanks, Doty." And to the hulking man, "Come on, I'll give you a ride home."

IT WASN'T WHAT he expected, but that didn't mean Big Ron hadn't asked someone else to do the dirty work for him. But on the ride back to the north side, the large man hadn't acted smug, hadn't given any impression of gloating. Instead he wanted to be reassured that Wager would take off the heat that had been making it hard to scrape up a living. "You gonna stop hassling with me now, right? You know now I didn't shoot you or nobody else, right?"

"You still haven't told me what I want to know about John Erle."

Framed in the car window, the broad face clenched. "I ain't got nothing to say about that."

"Then I guess we're right back where we were, Big Ron. You give my regards to your mother, will you?"

In the rearview mirror, the bulky, dark figure stared after Wager's car, unmoving, until it swung out of sight.

13

TO WAGER'S WAY of thinking, September was the finest month in Colorado: The afternoon thunderstorms of summer gradually ceased as the air grew cooler and drier; the sunlight had a pleasant little sting to it, a half-heat, half-chill that hinted of the coming icy winds; even the sky turned a deep blue that no other month had. Those kinds of days often carried into early October, too, but as that month passed the weather changed: unsettled, spells of harsher cold, splatters of rain; and late October always seemed to bring sleet or snow. At least Wager's memories of Halloween brought up pictures of jumping over slush puddles on the way to another doorbell, of being half blinded by an inky-smelling, rain-wet mask whose mouth hole was frayed from his damp breath, and of trying to guess if those bigger kids, sprinting noisily down the sidewalk and wearing smears of face paint or bandannas as token costumes, were friends who would join his group or enemies who would grab their sacks of candy and run off into the night of misrule and threat yelling, "Thanks for the treat, turkeys!"

But now, Wager's ghosts and goblins didn't wear masks and they didn't come during just one season; sometimes they were unknown but constantly nagging, like the killers of John Erle and Julio. Other times, they wore a name like Neeley and his so-called witness, Nelda Stinney. Yet Wager would just have to try and keep that spook clear of his thoughts because he wasn't being paid to worry about it. Wager's lawyer was, and he had to keep reminding himself of that.

Still, last night he had dreamed, and in that dream he wandered among a crowd of well-clothed people, begging help from deaf ears and feeling a shocking anxiety as he suddenly realized that he was naked and in a moment the rest of the world would realize it too and cover him with laughter and derision. And that moment came closer and closer with increasing panic. He woke himself up with his own hoarse voice before the worst happened, but he didn't need a shrink's license to recognize the feeling of helplessness he would have if he lost his job as a cop. A cop was what he was—he was a uniform, even more than being Gabe Wager or his mother's son. Dewing had warned him that his job was on the line, and he had heard those words, but it had taken a few weeks for the threat to really sink in. Because Neeley was a dirtball. He had gotten what was coming to him. Wager should not have to suffer any repercussions from doing his job. But he knew enough of the court system not to trust it. Juries and judges had done some strange things despite evidence or justice, and Wager did not at all enjoy the feeling of having his life and career in the hands of anyone other than himself. That included his lawyer or a possible jury, and it especially included Kolagny, who had been named the city's attorney in the case.

Dewing had said, "Kolagny doesn't seem to like you, Detective Wager."

"Kolagny doesn't know his butt from his elbow, either."

"Well, it would be better if he and I could put up a unified front against Heisterman. But it doesn't look like it's going to work out that way. In fact, Kolagny seems almost happy about you being sued. If you don't mind my asking, what'd you do to piss him off?"

"Told him I was tired of handing him four-square cases and then watching him throw away my work on bullshit plea bargains because he was too afraid to go into court and do his job."

"I guess that would do it, all right. OK—not to worry—we at least know what we can and can't count on from that direction."

Sighing, Wager turned from the gray light of the window. Its little rivulets of rain made tiny jumps down the glass and distorted the wet glare of taillights and the haze of spray in the streets below. The homicide office was busier than usual for this time of the morning: noisy with the steady rustle of papers and keyboards as well as the murmur of voices aimed into telephones, warm with the activities of people who found things to catch up on that would not take them away from the hot coffee and into the cold and wet of the streets. And maybe that was what Wager felt right now: an odd sense of depression at the vision of a wet, gray Denver outside, contrasting with the almost homelike familiarity and warmth of this ugly office. But the best cure for that kind of feeling was work, so he turned to the small stack of memos, court notices, transcripts, letters, forensic reports, requests, telephone messages, and even newsletters and advertisements that made up this way of life whose value had sharply increased.

The cold, damp weather had another effect: It had cooled off street activity and tempers, and the rumors and fears of gang wars had gone down with the temperature. Governor Harmon had shifted directions with practiced ease and now was reminding voters of the jobs he had created and the potholes he had filled. Even Gargan had stopped calling Wager, though now and then one of his news stories made sly reference to certain officers who were uncooperative with the fourth estate or who were being sued by people they had arrested. A third effect of the cold was that it made his trapezius sensitive to movement. The doctor said that wasn't supposed to happen, that there was no reason for it, and that he must be imagining it; so Wager didn't bother going back for his final checkup. It reminded him of the Marine Corps and the medical treatment he received for a sprung knee: two a.p.c.'s and a fifteen-mile hike. What the hell. It wasn't the doctor's shoulder. But it still twinged when his arm jumped out to catch the sudden tinny warble of his telephone.

"Wager, you know me."

He recognized the wheezing lurch of breathy words. "What do you have for me, Willy?"

"Gimme—gimme—gimme. You ain't even going ask how's my health. How's my day going."

"All right: How's your health and how's your day going? Now what do you have for me?"

"That's what I like about doing business with you, Wager. No time wasted on small talk, you know?"

"I wish I could say the same, Willy."

"Ha! Awright—I can take a hint. That boy you was asking about, he was working for Big Ron, all right. Lookout, holding the stash, deliveries, that kind of thing. I reckon ol' Ron he was planning to build up his business some more. Expand out a little, you know? But he back working by hisself, now, though."

"How long ago did Hocks start working for him?"

"Couple months, maybe. But nobody saying if he got shot by him. Nobody knows." He grunted. "Or at least that's what they say."

"Any rumors of Big Ron and anybody else pushing each other for territory?"

"Naw. But that shit go on all the time. You know, sometime worser'n others. Ain't heard about no gang war neither. Nothing more than the usual, leastwise." Another lurch of breath. "Oh, yeah—that boy, he had a street name: Doodle Bug."

"John Erle? Doodle Bug?" Street names, nicknames, and

gang names often indicated something about the bearer—a personality trait, a habit, even an historical event, like the one nicknamed "Rolaids" because, once in a shootout, he reached in his pocket for a shotgun shell and yanked out a package of antacids to jam into his weapon. "How'd he get that?"

"Say he was always doodling in this little notebook of his. Was really bugs about it. So that's what they called him."

"Who told you that, Willy?"

"One of my people he talked to this spic kid over on the west side. Arellano. Don't know his first name. Don't know him, neither. Just one of my people talked to him and that's what he say."

"Is Arellano in a gang?"

"He spic ain't he?"

"I could say the same thing about you, Willy."

"You couldn't say I was a spic—ha! Besides, I'm a one-man gang, Wager. I'm big enough to be my own gang. In so many ways! I just ain't wasting my time with all that Crips and Bloods shit." He paused to hock something untasty out of his throat. "My man say this Arellano belong to the L-one-oh-twos. That's all he know."

"OK. Now, one more thing."

"More! Man, you got to be the—"

"It's important, Willy."

"Yeah! Well, what's important to you might not mean shit to me."

"You shouldn't have any trouble with this one, unless you're losing touch with your own neighborhood."

"I ain't losing touch. Touch is what I got plenty of."

"Reach out and touch LaBelle Rhone for me. I tried her last address, but she'd already stiffed the landlord and moved on." He told Willy the old address. "Or didn't you know that she was back on the street?"

"She been back six months or more! Everybody knows that. Except maybe you—you just finding it out?"

"See if you can find out her new address, Willy."

"Shouldn't take me more'n ten minutes."

"Thanks."

"Don't want no thanks. Just remember I done you some favors."

It would be hard for Wager to forget if he wanted to: Willy would see to that the next time he or one of his had a problem with the law. And there was bound to be a next time, but that future issue went into the gray area where legality and justice didn't always coincide. Wager took a deep breath, gave Fullerton a call, and a half hour later had the information he needed: Arellano's first name was Guillermo, his street name Halconito, and the principal hangout for the L-102s was West 44th Avenue in the Chaffee Park neighborhood, the Estrellita Billiards Room. Wager also learned that the gang was one of the new ones, apparently unaffiliated so far with such larger organizations as the Westsiders or the Inca Boys, that the "L" in its name came from the street where most of the members grew up and still lived—Lipan—and that the 102 was the paragraph in the state criminal code that defined first-degree murder; he could not help learning that Denver, like the rest of the country, was following California's lead, that the latest LA census of gang membership estimated around 900 separate gangs or identifiable collectivities comprising an estimated 100,000 members, all or most of whom were armed. Fullerton was sending Wager some up-to-the-minute data about that despite the fact that Wager wasn't interested in LA.

"You never know when this kind of information might come in handy, Gabe."

Wager agreed and thanked the man; you had to take the bad with the good. He also took the elevator to the basement garage and headed out into the gray and cold streets of downtown.

AS A KID, Wager had not been allowed to go into billiard parlors; unlike cantinas they had been for men only, and the ladies of the barrio's families weren't welcome. And what was unsuitable for *una dama* wasn't suitable for their kids. This did not mean that Wager, as he moved into his early teen years, did not manage to spend some time at the local *salon* watching the *billar* players. He had even stroked a few cue balls himself, but—because the owner didn't trust kids jabbing cues across his expensive felt—had mostly dropped nickles into the pinball machines. What surprised him was how familiar the Estrellita felt with its welcome warmth and the odors of stale beer and strong tobacco, with its four green tables glowing under hooded lights and cigarette smoke, and crowded so close that people at neighboring tables had to take turns shooting. There was even a small bar advertising Cerveza Tecate and Dos Equis, among a variety of other brands including Coors on tap. The *ranchera* music, too, was familiar—this time some nasal voice wailing about how homesick he was for his house and family and sweetheart in beautiful Sinaloa. What was new were signs declaring *No Colores* and that everyone under thirty would have to show an ID to buy alcoholic beverages. Also new was the row of electronic games across the back wall: The pinball machines had been replaced by four video machines that beeped and roared and chattered electronic gunfire and explosions.

Wager didn't bother to use a barstool; the bartender already smelled cop. But he flashed his badge anyway—it was part of the ritual. "I'm looking for Guillermo Arellano, calls himself Halconito."

The bartender, a narrow face pitted with old smallpox scars, glanced at the row of noisy machines against the back wall. "Never heard of him."

"Right." He headed for the group of long-haired kids whose

baggy clothes looked like leftovers from a yard sale except they
were too dirty. Up close he could see that their stringy hair was
unwashed, too, and none of them looked as if they had a mother to
nag them about it. The tallest, a mouth-breather around fifteen or
sixteen, saw him headed their way and nudged the shorter kid
whose head was stuck in the hood of the Space Raiders machine.
He, too, fell silent and stared flatly as Wager approached, and
Wager congratulated himself on being a real detective: The
kid's shirt was pulled open across his bony and hairless chest
to show that tattoo of a spread-eagled bird whose wingtips brushed
each of his nipples. One nipple had a tiny gold ring through it.

"Halconito, right?" Wager showed his badge. The figures
moved closer together, a variety of heights and faces, but one
expression—suspicion.

"Are you Halconito?"

"Maybe. Why?"

"I'm with Denver Police. Need to ask you some questions
about a murder victim you know."

The five other kids had grouped themselves behind the one
with the tattoo, making it clear that he was their leader and that
his tattoo was as much their flag as his name. On the left hands
that Wager could see, he made out one large, dark tattoo per
knuckle: L, 1, 0, 2.

"Who's that, man? Who's *rapeadad*?" He made the word
sound something like "raped," a pun mixing the Spanish for
"snuff" and the Anglo for "raped." One of the slang terms when
Wager was a kid had been *tendido*—stretched out—but lan-
guage, too, changed.

"*Un negrito* named John Erle Hocks—*se llaman* Doodle
Bug." Wager added, "I heard a lot down at police headquarters
about you and the Lipan One-oh-twos. I heard you knew him."

"You heard about me?" Surprise mixed with pleasure; Arellano, who only came up to Wager's chin, seemed to swell another
inch or two. "You people know about the L-One-oh-twos?"

"Sure. It's police business to learn about *la gente,* no? You people are getting a name—people are starting to hear about the L-One-oh-twos."

"Fuckin' right, man! And a lot more people going to hear before long! Nobody be giving that L-One-oh-twos any shit, man, because they'll all know who we are!"

The chorus mumbled "That's right, man" and "You fuckin' right on!" Even the open-mouthed kid in the back, a foot or so taller than Wager, nodded hard, his stringy brown hair swaying back and forth limply across his face.

"*Por supuesto.* That's why I came to talk to you—ask you about Doodle Bug. Figured you'd be the ones to know."

Arellano shrugged, the gesture of a man who knew a lot more than anybody might guess. "So you find out who did him?"

"Not for sure. That's why I'm asking around about him. Asking those people who know enough about what's going on."

"Yeah—well—yeah. We knew him." He glanced over his shoulder. "Right?"

The heads nodded, but no one added anything.

"Do you know how he got that *mote*—Doodle Bug?"

"Sure. This little book he carried around, he was always writing in it. Big plans, man, a real *tiburón.* He was going to set up his own organization, like, and was always making notes about things to do, how to do it."

"What things?"

Some caution. "Things. Business. You know."

Wager was beginning to get the idea. "Did he say he was working for Big Ron?"

"Never heard of no Big Ron. Who's he?"

"Deals crack over in north Denver." A faint shuffle of unease among the group. Wager shook his head. "I don't care about that—I'm in homicide. My job's to find out who killed him." He gave Arellano another chance to add something, but the kid remained silent. "How'd you meet him?"

"Around. On the street. You know."

"But he was a black kid."

"We got friends—connections. All over the place. Some are black, some Anglo."

"Yeah." One of the medium-sized faces spoke up. "Even a couple Koreans. This is America, you know?"

They laughed loudly, and Wager smiled and nodded, too. The speaker was probably the group clown, the *comodin*. "Democracy—ain't it great!" That got another round of laughter, not quite so loud. "So Doodle Bug offered you a business deal—he was going to provide the stuff, and you could sell it and make a lot of money?"

That good feeling went as fast as it came. "Hey, man. I didn't say that."

"*No problema.* I didn't ask it. But if I knew something like that, I might be closer to his killer."

Arellano's grin made his face grow younger, bringing to Wager a sharp memory of one of those distant faces from the old Auraria barrio. It was a kid Wager had long ago forgotten and whose name he could not dredge up now. A distant relative in his family by somebody's bloodline.

"If there was a deal, it fell through. That's all I'm saying."

Wager nodded. "*Entiendo.*" He paused before leaving. "You ever hear of Julio Lucero or Roderick Hastings?"

The leader shook his head. Those standing behind him shook theirs.

"Lucero was shot a few weeks ago over on Thirty-fourth and Eliot. Killed."

"I heard about the shooting. I didn't know him, though."

"Thanks, men. '*Sta la vista.*"

"Yeah—*la vista.*"

THE NEXT TIME they saw each other might not be so friendly. Or maybe it would. Maybe one of the neighborhood do-gooders would reach the kids before they got so far in that Wager would be calling on them officially. Or trying to find their murderer. But that was a future he couldn't worry about, because the present was making its own demands. Back at his desk, he pulled the Hocks file and leafed through the crime scene analysis one more time. No mention of a notebook of any kind. Wager dialed the lab, managing to catch Gebauer before he took off for lunch.

"Notebook? What kind of notebook?"

"I don't know. A little one, probably; something he carried around with him. I hear Hocks was always writing in it. They called him Doodle Bug because he scribbled in it all the time."

"Can't recall it. If it's not in the site inventory or the list of personal possessions, it wasn't there."

"OK—thanks."

"Say, I heard you got shot."

"Nothing I'll get a medal for." Wager seldom thought of the wound now, except when he touched the slowly healing scab.

"Heard you're getting sued, too."

"That's worse than being shot."

"You leading an exciting life. Get the bastard who did it?"

"Shot me? No." Hadn't gotten the one who was suing him, either.

"Any idea who it was?"

"I think so. No proof yet."

"Well, if you need some help with him, or if I hear anything . . ."

Wager hardly knew Gebauer, but like almost every cop he'd talked with after the shooting, the man was ready to help Wager get vengeance. It was like a family: No matter how much you squabbled among yourselves, if someone from outside attacked, you were all against him. "Thanks."

His next call was to Arleta Hocks's work number, a convenience store on north Downing Street. She didn't have anything new to add to what she had already told Wager, but she was grateful that he was still looking for her son's killer. No, she didn't know of any notebook, but she would look through his belongings when she got off work this afternoon. Her mild voice was almost toneless, as if the death of her son had moved from a sharp pain to a constantly suffered throb of ache that was to be kept inside and borne alone. Yes, she would call right away if it was there.

His hand still on the telephone when it warbled. "For somebody who was acting in such a big hurry you sure ain't easy to reach."

"You've got me now, Willy. What is it?"

"That address you wanted—you know, LaBelle." He gave Wager the street number. "How long she gonna be there I don't know, but that's where she at right now."

"Got it—thanks, Willy."

"You heard what I done said about thanks."

Wager'd heard. He shoved his name across the location board to On Patrol and grabbed the elevator down to the garage.

It was a neighborhood of small brick houses separated from each other by narrow sidewalks that led to backyards. A few had squares of grass mowed, watered, and edged with what flowers had managed to survive this late in the year. Mostly chrysanthemums and petunias. The rest were fronted by yards either gleaming with standing water or churned into mud by busy kid feet. LaBelle's address was for a tiny brick duplex whose twin front doors shared the same small porch and central stairs. Brick bungalows crowded close on each side, one an unpainted red, the other a robin's egg blue that, even in the wet overcast, stung Wager's eyes. He rapped on the warped screen door and waited, listening for the sound of movement inside. Again, louder this time. After a third and even louder knock, the floor quivered with thudding heels.

"Yes? What you selling?"

"Hello, LaBelle. It's been a long time."

The face wrinkled to squint through the screen at Wager. "Who you? You that cop! What's his name—the one thinks he got solid gold balls."

"Wager." He put his badge case away. "How's tricks?"

"What you coming after me for? Whyn't you leave me alone—I ain't done nothing to you!"

He didn't want her to, either, but it looked like a lot had been done to her: a lot more years than the calendar said, and a lot less weight than he remembered. It could have been prison. It could be AIDS. It could be dope. Or maybe just a hard life that had ground her down like a worn knife blade. "I'm not here to bust you, LaBelle, not even for skipping out on your rent. I just want to talk about Roderick Hastings."

"I got nothing to say about that man!"

"I understand you saw him beat up a bartender over at JP's Lounge."

Something quivered beneath her defensive anger, and her voice rose in pitch. 'I don't know what you're talking about."

"Sure you do. It's in the police files—Officer Powers took your statement and you were called in as a witness against Hastings. Then you changed your story in court." Wager smiled. "We can go down and read the records if you want to. Or we can talk here."

"I didn't see nothing and you can't make me say I did!"

"That case is closed, LaBelle. Dismissed. Over. All I want is information about Hastings—where he lives, what he does, and who he does it with." He added, "Unless you think you owe him something. Is that it? He did something real nice for you so you're going to do him a nice favor now?"

Her face, clawed with wrinkles that put deep folds from her nose to the corners of her mouth, peered past Wager up and down the street. He noticed, hidden deep in the wiry hair curling at her temples, gray root that had grown out beneath the orange dye. She unlatched the screen door. "Come in. I don't want the whole neighborhood to see me talking to no cop in broad daylight."

The story was pretty much what Powers had told him: LaBelle had been hanging around outside JP's, waiting for any customers coming out at closing time, when she saw Hastings attack the bartender. "You ain't give me no Miranda warning— you can't make me go in court on this."

The Miranda didn't apply to witnesses, only to suspects, but LaBelle didn't have to know that. "I told you that case is closed. I'm after Hastings for something else."

"What?"

"He might have had something to do with a kid's death."

"Who he kill?"

"My cousin. Maybe. Maybe not."

The maybe didn't surprise her. As for it being Wager's cousin, well, in the world she knew people got killed every day, no matter whose cousin they happened to be. "He liked to hurt people. Him and them people he runs around with. Bloods. Say they hurt me if I go to court against him. Hurt me real bad." She nodded. "Would, too."

"Didn't Officer Powers offer you protection?"

"Shit! Ain't no protection against them. They wants to get you, they gonna get you. In jail, out of jail, ain't no protection gonna stop them!"

"Who are some of the people he hangs around with?"

She gave him some names that he would have to check with Fullerton—Ball Peen, Rubberhead, Wild Bill. More important, she told him where Hastings and his friends usually gathered. "They got them a place in that apartment house over at Sixteenth and Washington. Call it the snake ranch. You going over there?"

"Probably sooner or later. Why?"

"They gonna shoot you dead, then."

"Why's that, LaBelle?"

"Same reason they beat up that bartender. Maybe same reason they shoot your cousin: They got a business to protect and they don't want nobody to know nothing about it."

Wager studied the dark brown eyes that looked back at him from under lids that were wrinkled and dry from some kind of allergy or disease. "How'd you know about it?"

She shrugged. "I see things. I hear things." A snort. "Lots of men likes to talk after they fuck, you know? That's when they feel like they really somebody." They were both silent a moment. "That cop over in District Two—Powers?—he think Hastings and that bartender they just had a dustup." She shook her head. "More'n that went down. That bartender, he took some stuff on commission and then went and used it all—couldn't pay Hastings what he owed him. I bet your cousin done it, too. I bet your cousin try and short Hastings, too. I bet you got a dopehead in your own fambly!"

That was all she could or would tell him, but it wasn't all she meant. Wager, on the drive back to police admin, kept seeing the malignant laughter in the woman's eyes as she accused Julio of using drugs. Not that she had anything against his cousin, but it was Wager she felt triumph over; the cop who had arrested her in the past was now learning that he wasn't any better than she was, that if she was dirt, so was he and all his family. And Wager knew that the reasons she had talked so freely to him about Hastings was not just out of revenge against those who had threatened her but as a way of getting even with him, too.

HE WAS TRYING to explain that to Elizabeth later that evening. She had a rare night without campaign meetings or party functions or neighborhood electioneering; and they had gone to his apartment for a change of environment—and to get away from her telephone—to cook spaghetti, toss a salad, find some quiet time to share a glass of wine or two. But of course what they talked about were the very things they were trying to escape: the election and Wager's cases.

"Dennis Trotter's taken a leaf from the governor's campaign."

"What's that?" Wager mopped at the remains of the sauce with a hunk of bread. Liz had been right: Trotter had emerged as the strongest challenger for her council seat; Wager had seen his large glossy posters in yards all over the district.

"Crime. 'Police and citizens working together to stop crime.' That's his main theme." Her tone expressed disgust. "It's his way of shifting attention from the stadium issue."

It was also a bunch of election-year crap—cops learned before they were out of their probationary term that damn few, if any, civilians ever came to their aid. That's why an Officer Down call took precedence over everything else: The down cop was always alone. But he didn't tell that to Elizabeth; despite the good food and the snug sound of rain whipping at the balcony doors, she would rise to argue with his cynicism. Instead he told her about Roderick Hastings and Julio and what LaBelle had said.

"It's corrupting an entire generation, Gabe. It's horrible—it's like AIDS, spreading and destroying. And it's happening mostly among kids and young people."

"It's their choice, Liz. Nobody makes them use it or deal it."

"Nobody except the greed of our society, and our callousness toward our own children."

"That puts the blame everywhere and nowhere. Each one has to make his own choice—nobody can do it for them."

"How do you make an eleven- or twelve-year-old kid understand that, Gabe? Especially one who lives in a world of fear and intimidation in his neighborhood, in his school, often in his own home. He's going to join a gang for survival and he's going to do what he sees the other members of that gang doing." It genuinely hurt her to learn from Wager some of the uglier aspects of life in her city, and that pain was in her voice. "It's a reversion to tribalism—our children are losing the sense that we're a civilized people, that we should all live together in our city and that we can do it. Instead they form tribes whose purposes are defense from and attack against the other tribes. It's a horrible vision of the death of a civilization, Gabe."

Which meant that one of the first things to do was to make the world a little safer place—and that's what Wager's job was and what he was trying to accomplish. "Julio was not a user. The autopsy showed no traces in his system and no marks on his body. And I don't believe he was in a gang or that he was dealing."

"Then why was he killed?"

"Because he was some kind of threat to Hastings's racket— or maybe Hastings believed he was."

"What does Detective Golding think about that?"

"Golding doesn't think." Wager had told the man what he was working on, but Golding had only nodded earnestly and said what a good idea it was but that he would wait and see if anything turned up to corroborate Wager's theory. "He wants somebody to step up and admit they shot Julio."

"Have you asked Julio's mother about it? About any possibility that he could have been involved?"

No, Wager hadn't. It wasn't something he would even mention to Aunt Louisa because he didn't want the woman to know that Wager even held such a suspicion about her dead son. His own mother would be the same way: protective of Julio's name and of her sister's, angry at the idea of defaming the dead boy and his family with evil thoughts. All the warmth and appreciation that she had shown Wager for his having been thoughtful enough to call and warn her about his earlier wound would be blown away by his—in her eyes—acting like a cop and virtually accusing an innocent murdered child of a crime. "It's not something she'd know about." But who would? And where else might Julio have seen Hastings other than on the job out at DIA? Where had Julio gone, and who with, in the week or so before he was killed? Maybe Aunt Louisa knew that, at least.

14

FOR A CHANGE Fullerton was willing to talk over the telephone. "Jeez, I'd like to have you down for a cup of coffee, Gabe, and we could go over this in some detail. But I got to be in court in fifteen minutes."

"That's OK, Norm. No problem, really."

"OK. Did you get a chance to look at those LA demographics yet?"

"Yeah—thanks for the info. A hundred thousand gang members, that's a damned scary number."

"And growing every day. They really have a recruiting program. They're going after the nine- and ten-year-olds now. And those kids think they're living in TV land, you know? Have no real idea at all about what killing somebody means."

"Norm. I've got some names for you. Maybe you can give me some leads." He repeated what he got from LaBelle yesterday afternoon. "Any sound familiar?"

"Rubberhead. That's got to be James Sleppy. Last I heard he went down to Cañon City three or four years ago for assault with intent. Like his name says: crazy—beat his girlfriend half to death with a two-by-four because she drank his orange juice.

She didn't want to testify against him, but they were living together so the DA could arrest him under the domestic violence law without her complaint. I didn't know he was out."

"That wasn't one of Kolagny's cases, was it?"

"No. I don't think so. I can look it up for you if you want me to."

"Never mind." Wager checked the spelling of Sleppy's name so he could pull the man's jacket.

"Don't know which Wild Bill you want—there's a lot of people around with that name. Ball Peen, now there's a case: likes to work people over with a ball-peen hammer's how he got his name. We thought we had him on murder one—splintered some guy's head—but his lawyer got him off on self-defense. Heisterman."

"Who?"

"Heisterman. A real shyster—works for the gangs. Gets big bucks for it, too. Son of a bitch is indirectly guilty of half a dozen murders that his clients committed after he got them off."

"Heisterman?"

"Yeah. You know him?"

"I suspect I'm going to run across him."

Attorney Dewing found it interesting, too. "He's a lawyer for the gangs?"

"Fullerton knows him. Says he's a favorite with the OGs who can afford him. Bloods or Crips, makes no difference as long as they pay." Wager asked, "Could that be grounds to dismiss the suit?"

"No, Heisterman's not the plaintiff. Neeley is. So I don't see how it changes things materially. But it is interesting—it tells me more about the opposition. By the way, did I tell you Heisterman's trying to move the trial date up? Wants to have it within three weeks."

Three weeks. Wager felt his chest tighten. "No. You didn't."

"Claims that the current trial date is causing his client emotional damage that is aggravating to his severe physical injuries."

"What kind of crap is that?"

"A crappy argument, but an argument: increasing mental stress caused by a sense of the injustice of his injuries, plus now an accusation that we're trying to delay the trial."

"Who's delaying it?"

"Well, I did ask for a continuance. I want to see if we can find some other witnesses who might have been overlooked by the shooting team. If they missed one, they could have missed others."

That was true, given Maholtz was the team commander. "Is that Heisterman's rush? He's afraid you might find someone?"

"Maybe. I don't know. But he asked for the case to be moved up before I asked for the delay. The judge informed me when I petitioned him—in fact, he was just about to call me in to see if I had any objections to the plaintiff's petition."

"What the hell's going on, Counselor?"

"You know what I know, Detective Wager."

Which was scary because it wasn't much. "So will the date be moved up?"

"I doubt it—with two conflicting petitions, the judge will probably let the original trial date stand." Wager felt his breathing loosen with relief. "Unless one of us comes up with something a lot more compelling than our current arguments."

IF THE FACT that Heisterman was a gang lawyer was interesting for Dewing, it was bothersome for Wager. It bothered him that Neeley should have Heisterman for his lawyer both at his trial that he lost as well as now; it especially bothered him that Heisterman might have connections to Hastings through his defense of Ball Peen.

Sitting at the small worktable in the Records section, he

combed through the thick files on James "Rubberhead" Sleppy and Ball Peen, whose mother, thirty-two years ago, had named her baby Kwame N'Kruma Mitchell. They, too, had Los Angeles backgrounds and a series of arrests and convictions that mirrored Hastings's life. Which, Wager guessed, was one reason they called each other brother. Their attorneys' names, of course, didn't show up in these files; to learn those, Wager would have to comb through court records, but it wouldn't surprise him to learn that Rubberhead's lawyer had also been Heisterman. And that was another thing that bothered Wager: if he talked to Heisterman about these other clients it could— would—be made to look as if Wager had a conflict of interest because of the Neeley suit. Especially since Julio's case wasn't even his. It was like a goddamn chess game; Wager felt himself being closed out of large areas of the board by moves that he had no control over. Yet he also had the feeling that the reasons for Julio's murder lay in this area just somewhere off his fingertips . . . that with a little more digging, with a break or two . . . But now, where Hastings was concerned, he would have to walk like a cat.

AUNT LOUISA WAS ready for him, armed with almond cookies and a pot of coffee. The sharpness of her grief had dulled into an air of resignation, and she spoke softly in a way that reminded Wager of John Erle's mother; he guessed that both women had a way of hiding things inside, of dwelling in silence on their hurts. "It's good to see you, Gabe. You're looking good."

"Thanks, Aunt Louisa. These *galletas* are good—*muy sabrosas*." Actually, they tasted sort of dry and sugarless, the way a lot of Mexican *dulces* did. But what else could he say? The coffee, as usual, really was tasty. "I've got to ask you some questions about Julio. Things you maybe didn't remember earlier."

"I understand, Gabe." She settled herself a little more heavily at the other end of the small sofa. On the wall, freshly framed, smiled an enlargement of Julio's yearbook picture; a cross made out of narrow strips of white felt was stuck to an upper corner, and on a small table under the photograph, a *vela* flickered in its red glass.

"I need to know exactly what happened the time Julio quit his job out at DIA. Anything he said to you at all, anything you might have wondered about, everything that happened." He added, "Start with, say, the week before he quit—did he come home from work upset in any way?"

Her dark eyes went to the photograph, and Wager saw a faint tremor in the coffee that filled her cup. She sipped some out and put the cup safely on its saucer. "I'll try."

At first there wasn't much different from what she had told him a few weeks ago, and she was apologetic. She wanted to give him important details that she believed he would like to hear. He had to remind her several times that wasn't the idea—just tell him what happened, no matter how small or unimportant something might seem. Even close her eyes if that helped her recall things. Just try to remember anything and everything— there wasn't anything special he was seeking, he said. Which wasn't entirely true; he had an idea, and it gave him some direction for the gently probing questions he asked now and then. But the story was Aunt Louisa's—her reliving of the last weeks of her son's life, and the more she talked about it the more she recalled, and, moving back and forth in time and place as association fed her memory, she finally gave Wager a fairly clear picture.

Julio had been upset even before he stopped going to work; she had forgotten about that until Wager asked. About a week before, maybe a Thursday—he stopped going on the following Wednesday—he came home unsmiling and restless, but he wouldn't say anything to her except it was nothing for her to worry about. Just some stuff at work. He went off the next morning, it must have been Friday, looking tired and said he hadn't slept much. But she didn't think anything of that—she had restless nights too every now and then.

"Do you know how much money he was making out there?"

"Money? Yes. He was doing real good. He made almost a hundred and eighty dollars a week. He gave me his paycheck to help with the bills and didn't keep much for himself at all. Said he didn't have nothing to spend it on anyway."

"Did he have any other income you know of?"

She shook her head, puzzled. "Where would he get it?"

Wager changed direction. "What did Julio do over the weekend before he died?"

Well, come to think of it, not much. A lot of times he'd go to a movie with a friend or by himself or watch sports on TV. But, she remembered now, he didn't even pay much attention to the television, she even said something to him about a program and he didn't even know what he was watching. It was like he had been asleep staring at the screen.

"Did he say anything about anyone? Mention any names at all?"

"No . . . but whenever the telephone rang, he'd ask me to answer it. Ask who it was before he would talk. Remember, I already told you about that?"

"Was there anyone he did talk with?"

"Anthony. That's his friend. The one he'd usually go to the movies with. He talked to him a couple times, but I don't know what about. I didn't want to listen, you know, and Julio wouldn't talk loud."

On Monday of the week he quit work, Julio came home upset again—or at least worried. In fact, she asked him if he was feeling all right, if he was feeling sick or something, he was so quiet. But he said no.

"Did he talk to Anthony then?"

No. That was when he stopped answering the telephone altogether; and the next couple of mornings, he didn't even want to go to work but he wouldn't say why. She had asked him, but all he said was he didn't like the job anymore—that all they had him do was move junk around and pick up scraps and it was a big waste of time. When he got the job they told him he would be learning a trade, you know, carpentry or cement work, that kind of thing. But they didn't teach him nothing so he wanted to quit, and finally he did. . . .

The interview took almost three hours, and when Wager finally went down the front steps of the bungalow, his trapezius ached but not from being shot. They both ached from tension. It had turned out to be as much therapy for his aunt as informative for Wager, and he felt drained from the effort to hold that narrow balance between making her remember and talk and preventing her from collapsing into tears. *Una llorona.* Even though she had a right to be sad, Wager was glad to be out of that small living room with its shadowy corners and the flickering candle and the almost suffocating air of ceaseless mourning.

It was a block and a half to Anthony's and nearing dinnertime when Wager knocked on the door of a house almost identical to Julio's. The homes along the wet, tree-lined street looked as if they had been built from the same plan: all brick, all small. Some were painted tan, others white, still others brighter colors like that Day-Glo purple house on the corner. Any differences in shape or size had grown gradually as rooms or even floors were added by one generation or another.

A kid in his mid-teens answered the door and nodded when Wager identified himself and asked if he was Anthony Ortiz.

"Got a few minutes to talk, Anthony? I'd like to ask you a few questions about Julio Lucero."

"Sure!" He came out onto the porch and shut the door against the cold air. "I don't know what else I can tell anybody."

"Have you talked to any other detectives?"

"Yeah. This guy came by a couple weeks ago was a detective, but I couldn't tell him much."

Wager was surprised that Golding had been ahead of him. And mildly piqued. "Did he ask you how Julio felt about his job out at DIA?"

"No. Just when I saw him last, if he was in a gang. If I could give him the names of other kids he ran around with, like that. If I had any idea who wanted to kill him." He shook his head. "I didn't. Still don't. It's . . . I don't know . . . something like that just makes the world seem like it's full of crap, you know?"

More crap than this young man knew about—or, if he was lucky, would ever know about. "Did Julio have a lot of money after he started working out there?"

"A lot of money?" Anthony's black eyebrows pulled together and he shook his head. "He had a little, but it wasn't a lot. He kept some out of his paycheck, but a lot of it he gave to his mother. He liked to think he was paying for his room and board, since he was working full-time. I guess she put it in the bank for him or used it for groceries, I don't know."

"Did Julio ever talk to you about his job before he was killed?"

"Yeah. He didn't like it. He said he was thinking of quitting, but he knew his mother wouldn't want him to."

"Did he say why he wanted to quit?"

"Said they weren't teaching him anything. He thought it was a way to learn construction, you know? Learn a trade."

"Did he say anything about being afraid of somebody out there? Or worried about somebody?"

Anthony reached up and scratched under the small pigtail of straight brown hair gathered over the nape of his neck. "He did kind of say something like that. Not that he was really afraid of the guy but that some guy was hassling him at work—giving him a hard time, like."

"Did he say why?"

Anthony shook his head. "Just a black guy. Didn't like him because Julio was *la raza*, you know?"

Wager nodded. "Anything else? Anything at all you can remember about that?"

"Well, he wanted this guy to lay off him. Said if he didn't he was going to get him in trouble."

"The black guy was going to get Julio in trouble?"

"No—the other way around. Julio'd do for him."

"What was Julio going to do?"

Another shrug. "He didn't say. Just get the guy in trouble."

"Did you talk with him after he quit his job?"

"No. I didn't even know he'd quit. He never got home from work until late, and I work four days a week over at McDonald's after school. I called a couple times but he wasn't home. His mother always answered and said he wasn't home. I don't know where he was."

Wager asked a few more questions about other people Julio might have confided in, but Anthony had no names other than the ones Wager had already interviewed at West High: Ricky Gonzales, Henry Solano. When he dropped out of school, Julio had dropped out of what social life he led. No, he'd never heard Julio mention anyone called Roderick Hastings or Big Ron. No, he'd never ever heard of Julio getting mixed up with any gang, either in school or after he quit. Wager thanked Anthony and left a business card in case he remembered anything else.

15

SERGEANT BLAINEY, like most of the cops in District Two, had the night shift. Wager's telephone call caught the man as he was reporting in. "Doodle Bug? That's what they called him?"

"Because he was always writing in a notebook."

"I ain't asked around about any Doodle Bug."

"I'd like to find that notebook, too."

"Awright. I see what I can find out." There was something else on his mind. "What's this I hear you pulled in Big Ron Tipton for shooting at you? He the one?"

"I talked to him about it. I don't think he did it himself."

"But maybe he knows something about it?"

"Yeah. I do believe he might. Have you heard anything?"

"No. But I'll keep my ears open. Keep my eyes open, too, for that worthless bastard."

His next call was to Mrs. Hocks. A girl answered and said she wasn't home right now but could she take a message.

Wager identified himself and asked, "Is this Coley or Jeanette?"

"Coley."

"Did your mother say anything about finding a notebook that your brother liked to write in?"

"No, sir."

"Well. I asked her if she'd mind looking for it. It might be important. Could you tell your mother I called and asked if she remembered to look for John Erle's notebook?"

"Yes, sir."

He hung up and made a note to call again—the little girl might or might not remember to give her mother the message. The electric clock on the wall over a bulletin board crowded with notices and wanted flyers told him that Adamo might be reporting in about now, and he punched in those numbers. The V & N detective, sounding rushed, answered.

"Hi, Gabe. I'm doing what I can with what I got about Big Ron. Apparently nobody was checking on him the night you were shot. Schuyler says he spent most of his time at that accident call and then responded to your call—how're you doing, by the way?"

"Fine, Walt. But that's not what I need this time. What can you tell me about a Roderick Hastings? Fullerton tells me he and some others are probably helping the CMG Bloods set up a crack ring." He gave Adamo the nicknames of Hastings's friends. "Wesloski says he doesn't have anything on him, but I just heard on the street that Hastings and his people are dealing big."

That put Wager into Adamo's territory, and he got interested. "Who'd you hear that from?"

"A hooker. She sounded pretty sure of her facts."

The line was silent a moment. "The CMGs bit fits—like I told you, we've netted up a couple members of that little bunch lately. But Hastings and these other names, nothing."

"She sounded pretty sure, Walt." He thought a minute. "What about these names—they work out at DIA with Hastings." He read off the list of the man's coworkers at the airport site.

"No. DIA? You say this Hastings works out there?"

"Yeah. Does that mean anything?"

" . . . Maybe . . . Word is, there's been a lot of stuff available out there for a long time. Uppers and crack, mostly. A big construction job always has its share of users—you know, young guys with good pay and nothing to spend it on except cards and hell-raising. But we've started hearing some real stories about DIA. Construction accidents with stoned workers, that sort of thing." He added, "As far as I know, we haven't had a chance to look into it. My section hasn't, anyway. Of course there might be some undercover work going on out there; I wouldn't necessarily know about that. We got a big push against crack houses right now. We got all we can handle with that."

And, Wager was well aware, there was an election coming up. Citizens with votes would read about the crack houses being cleaned up in their neighborhoods, but any drug activity out at DIA was a long way from the polling booth.

"If you do hear anything about Hastings or those other names, would you let me know?"

"You got it."

THAT ELECTION WAS three weeks off, and Elizabeth's brief respite was over. She was spending this evening at the studio of the public television channel as one of the panel of candidates for city council. The interviewer was a man whose aviator glasses emphasized his triangular face. He talked through his nose and asked questions that tended to be longer than the answers he got from the half-circle of faces he addressed. Most likely, Wager thought, because it kept the camera on him. Elizabeth was the third from the right, and Wager—being absolutely objective—thought her answers were sharp, clear, direct, and at times really witty. She was the best of the bunch. She did a good job answering and even clarifying some of the more convoluted questions from the self-important moderator, and Wager found himself feeling damned proud of her.

Trotter, Liz's main opponent, was tanned, handsome in a blow-dried sort of way, and smiled a lot; he made a lot of jokes and bowed slightly toward Liz when he addressed her directly, calling her "Miz Voss." Wager didn't like him. But the audience did, and the moderator, responding to a kindred soul, bantered back and forth with him, repeated several times that the Chamber of Commerce supported him, and gave him plenty of time to talk about uniting the citizens and the police to stop crime. He believed that the Broncos deserved a brand-new stadium but couldn't say much about how it should be financed except that it would be a good thing for Denver's image and the city would benefit by it. To which the moderator agreed.

When the program ended—with a steady stare by the moderator into the camera—Wager turned off his set and glanced at the time: ten o'clock. Liz would make it home in about an hour, exhausted and faced with a 7:00 AM breakfast meeting. Wager, on the other hand, was on his way out again. He paused long enough to leave a message on her telephone answerer telling her he liked the job she did. He didn't tell her that he was going out on the street; he wasn't planning on being shot again.

The apartment house on the corner of 16th and Washington was red brick and trimmed with white stone over the doors and windows. A narrow band of white stone marked each of the building's four floors, and the corners of those bands had white stone carvings: flowers of some kind that hung out to catch the grime of the city. Wager had once asked somebody why so many of Denver's buildings were brick or stone or stucco; the answer had been the fire code. The town, originally of log shanties and wood-frame shops, had come close to burning down so many times that toward the end of the nineteenth century, the city fathers decreed that henceforth all building would be in masonry. It not only helped fireproof the city but also made a couple of new millionaires: councilmen who had bought out a local brickworks the day before the issue was put on the public agenda.

The buildings had not only been erected against fire, many of them had been built to stay. The Washington Arms was one that stayed, and it seemed to be kept in pretty good shape. At least it didn't smell of anything worse than dust, and the solid walls and deep. slightly worn carpeting sealed off both the outside noise as well as any coming from the apartments. Wager walked up the silent, cushioned stairs to the second floor; apartment nine was at the end of the hall next to a large window with a Fire Exit sign over it. That would give the occupants two ways in and out of the building if they needed them. He knocked, the rap muffled by the thick wood of the heavy door.

He could not tell if anyone peeked through the security eye in the center of the door, but the time it took before the first lock rattled hinted that he had been appraised. The sound moved down the doorframe as other locks clattered, and a final bolt slid back at the knob. The door swung open to show a large figure wearing lime green slacks and a silver-and-black mesh T-shirt that emphasized the bulge of shoulder and chest muscles. His head was shaved up the sides and back, and the long hair on the front and top—woven into narrow woolen strands—was gathered together in a bunch that sprouted straight up like a clutch of black yarn. "He'p you?"

Wager dangled his badge over his forefinger. "I'm looking for Roderick Hastings. He in?"

Across the room, glowing with red indicator lights and the flicker of three or four illuminated monitors, a large sound system pumped out soft music: something in cool jazz that didn't have a clear melody but seemed to drift with the saxophone player's mood. "I'll see."

The door closed and a minute or two later opened again. Hastings, flat nose and all, scowled at him. "What you want?"

"I've got a few more questions to ask about Julio Lucero, Mr. Hastings. Maybe you can answer them."

"Maybe. What you want to know?"

"You were already on the job when he was hired, that right?"

"Yeah."

"How long have you worked out at DIA, Mr. Hastings?"

"Me? About a year, maybe a little more. Why?"

"Just trying to fill in the picture. Did Julio ever say anything to you about being afraid of somebody out there?"

"Afraid? What for?"

"That's what I'm trying to find out." Wager smiled. "He told a friend of his that he was having some trouble with you, Mr. Hastings. Any truth to that?"

"Trouble? I didn't have no trouble with him. What kind of trouble you hear about?"

"Just trouble."

"Somebody giving you a line."

"But you did have some trouble over at JP's Lounge, right?"

He thought that over, eyes staring into Wager's. "That wasn't much of anything. I wouldn't call that trouble."

"The charges were dropped for lack of evidence?"

"That's why it wasn't no trouble. All this got something to do with that Lucero kid?"

"Might. I'm still trying to put things together."

"That because he was your cousin?"

"Where'd you hear about that?"

"Was in the newspaper a while back." A tiny gleam in the dark eyes, but his voice remained carefully neutral. "Along with something about you getting sued. How's that going?"

"My lawyer's taking care of that," Wager said carelessly. "Happens all the time." Then he chanced something. "Do you know Charles Neeley?"

Another pause. "I heard the name around. Why?"

"Just wondered. What about Big Ron Tipton? Know him?"

Hastings shook his head. "No. Who's he?"

"Lives over on the north side. Deals a little crack."

"What's that mean?"

"Deals crack?"

"No. You asking me about him. What's it mean do I know him?"

"Doesn't mean anything if you don't know him. You never had a run-in with Lucero?"

"Never."

"OK, Mr. Hastings. Thanks for your help."

The man smiled slightly with his lips. "Anytime." The door closed softly.

WAGER'S ALARM PULLED him out of bed groggy enough to scratch at his itching wound before he realized what he was doing. The sting of breaking flesh reminded him and he said "damn" and pressed a Kleenex hard against the bleeding scab. The shower started it bleeding again, and as he shaved he held a wad of toilet paper over the wound. It didn't stop bleeding, but he managed to put an awkward bandage over it to keep the color from seeping through his shirt. It was a lousy way to start the day, and he hoped it wasn't an omen; but at least the rain had stopped, and even the thick clouds seemed to be lightening. He checked on duty via radio and asked the clerk if there were any urgent messages for him.

"Negative, Detective Wager. Some telephone messages but nothing marked urgent."

"OK—I'm headed out to DIA and I'll be in the office about ten."

"Ycssir."

He pulled his rental car into a vacant square of dirt in front of the trailer marked D & S Contractors. The door stood open but the office was empty; Wager lounged against the doorframe and looked for Tarbell's figure among what he could see of the almost completed buildings. Finally he spotted the man walking his way, wearing a hardhat and carrying a clipboard aflutter with papers.

"Morning, Officer. What can I do for you?"

"Just a few more questions, if you've got time, Mr. Tarbell."

He glanced at the watch nestled in the thick, sun-reddened hairs on the back of the wrist. "Jesus, I wish you guys could do it all at once and get it over with. I really got a shitpot full of work to do."

"Has another detective been out talking to you?"

"Yeah, week or so ago. Goldman, Golding. Something like that. Me and the crew." His irritation increased. "You going to want to talk to them again too?"

"I don't think so."

He nodded, a little relieved. "All right—but let's keep it short. OK?"

"When did Roderick Hastings start working for you?"

"Hastings. He was one of our first hires. That was when we set up operations here. That would be about eighteen months ago."

"Just what does your company do?"

"Disposal and salvage. That's what the D and S stand for. We've subcontracted to clean up the site. That's what the boys do—gather up packing materials, discarded supplies and equipment, odds and ends that other contractors want to get rid of but that we can salvage."

"So your workers go all over the site."

"Sure. Everywhere there's stuff to pick up. Have to."

"Did you ever hear of any trouble between Lucero and Hastings?"

The man shook his head, the stubby bill of his white hard hat wagging back and forth. "They could have had some words, but as long as it didn't interfere with their work, I wouldn't have heard about it." His eyes widened slightly. "Why? You think Hastings had something to do with that boy's death?"

"Not necessarily. Does he have a locker here? A place where he keeps his street clothes?"

"No. None of the boys do. If they change on the job, it's in their cars or behind a trailer."

"Do you know which car is Hastings's?" Wager nodded toward the line of vehicles in an uneven row and glinting in the weak light of the thinning overcast.

"That Honda over there, I believe." He pointed to a red sedan. "Listen, this is kind of upsetting. Do you really suspect him? You really think he might have done it?"

"I don't know, Mr. Tarbell. I'm just checking things out."

The man's pale red eyebrows pulled together. "I don't know that much about Hastings. He's just one of the laborers."

"Isn't he a bit old to be in the youth program?"

"He didn't come through them. He showed up asking for work and I put him on." He added, fairly, "He's been a good worker. And like I say, I've never heard of him having any troubles with anybody."

"Is he always around when you need him?"

"Around? Sure—I mean, I don't see the crew all the time. I've got the deskwork to keep up with. But I start them on a job first thing in the morning and then check around ten or eleven. Then after lunch, if there's another job, I start them there. And I always check around three to see how things are going—get some idea of the next day's work. I haven't had any trouble with Hastings doing his work. I got to say that."

Wager thanked Tarbell and asked him not to tell Hastings about his visit. On the way to his car, he strolled by the red Honda and glanced in through the windows. The seats were empty, though a lunch box and large metal thermos rested on the floor of the rider's side. There was nothing to be readily seen by the casual observer that would support a search warrant.

Wager would very much like to have the lab boys run trace tests on the vehicle's trunk, but he'd need more probable cause before he could get that. And looking for probable cause, given the Neeley lawsuit, could be tricky for Wager. But he did write down the license number—a Denver code—before he headed back to the admin building.

16

BURIED AMONG THE routine messages waiting for him were two pink telephone slips that warranted quick attention. One, dated earlier this morning, told him to "Call Counselor Dewing." The other said "Mrs. Hocks called." The Please Call Back box was double-checked, Esther's shorthand for "caller said important." The time and date of receipt on that was yesterday afternoon, and Wager cursed himself for forgetting to tell the clerk that he was waiting for the call. Wager dialed the number—the convenience store—and a man said that she hadn't come in yet.

"What time do you expect her?"

"Seven AM."

The clock over the cluttered bulletin board said it was well after nine. "Did she call in sick?"

"Officer, that woman didn't call in at all; I had to call her. And even her kids said they didn't know where she was."

"Thanks. If she does come in, tell her I was trying to reach her, will you?"

"After I tell her she's fired."

Wager, too, tried her home number, but there was no answer.

A weekday, the girls should be in school by now. He shifted his attention to Counselor Dewing.

"Detective Wager, have you been poking your nose into this case?"

"Which case?"

"The only case you and I have a mutual interest in right now—Neeley."

"No." Then he remembered. "I did search CCIC to see if Nelda Stinney's name turned up, but it didn't. Why?"

"Don't even do that! Heisterman called me bright and early this morning to complain that you were threatening to harass his client, you were close to tampering with his witnesses, and that any such action on your part, no matter how inconsequential, would result in immediate and severe criminal charges. They would, too." She added, "Of course if you do tamper, you won't have to worry about saving your job—you won't have it, and that would include your pension. You still there?"

" . . . Yeah, I'm here. I just don't know what in the hell Heisterman's talking about. I haven't talked to, called, or communicated with Neeley or Stinney in any way."

"Well, don't—and I mean it, Detective Wager. Not with Neeley, not with Stinney, not with anyone who might know them. Don't do anything that could possibly be construed as a direct or indirect communication with them. Hard as it may be, you have to trust me to handle things. You stay the hell out of it."

That was her repeated message and summed up what she had to say, even when he kept asking questions. No, Heisterman had not yet made any formal claim of harassment or tampering. No, he did not speak to any specific instance. He just telephoned a warning, and Dewing was relaying it. With emphasis: Do not screw up.

For a few minutes after she hung up, Wager didn't hear any of the clatter and chatter of the office; he was going back over the last few days trying to remember the people he had spoken with and the subjects they'd discussed. Heisterman . . .

Neeley . . . the CMG Bloods . . . that's where the connection had to be—Roderick Hastings, maybe Big Ron Tipton, they both had ties to the Bloods. Somewhere in there . . . Either one of them or someone Wager had talked to who knew one of them . . . Perhaps a name he'd asked about, a question he'd asked someone . . . Wager felt his ideas slowly begin to come together in that way they sometimes did: moving from question to possibility, shifting the angles of possibility a little here, a touch there, and then with one of those tingling starts, knowing! And knowing that—

"Any homicide detective."

Wager jotted down the tail end of his fragmented thought on a memo pad and grabbed the radio resting in its battery pack. The call was to District Two and wasn't unusual for that city quadrant—another body had been found.

THE FAMILIAR YELLOW tape closed off one mouth of the alley, a patrol car with flashing lights blocked the other end. It was a slit between the backs of tall redbrick buildings: warehouses and clothing manufacturers, furniture stores and office suppliers, distributors, wholesalers. Already cluttered with dumpsters, fire escapes, and scarred concrete loading docks, the narrow space was even more crowded by those whose job was to clean up after the city's violence and death: the policemen and crime scene technicians, the waiting Cadaver Removal Service team, a television crew busy unloading from a Jeep station wagon, Gargan—whose mouth Wager could see in action as he approached it. It wasn't the importance of the victim that drew the media, Wager knew; it was just that the body had been found during working hours and close enough to the media offices so it couldn't be ignored. A handful of civilians with nothing better to do clustered across the street to peer through the traffic being waved past.

Wager, his badge recognized by the patrolman guarding the tape, nodded to Lincoln Jones. The tall lab photographer was just finishing some long shots of the scene with the video recorder before shifting to the Speed Graphic he liked for the stills. He had once told Wager that none of the newer cameras the department could afford worked as quickly or picked up as much detail as the bulky old box.

"Any ID?"

Jones shook his head. "Don't know. Woman, middle-aged."

Wager nodded. Gebauer, ballpoint pen busy at the crimescene form on his clipboard, looked up as Wager approached. "Beating death. Pretty ugly."

It was, but that wasn't what gave Wager that sudden ache in the gut. The face, twisted unnaturally over the bleeding shoulder that poked through the torn cloth of her dress, was battered and spongy. One eye bulged like a boiled egg from its socket. The skin of the cheeks and jaw was crusted with dried blood and oddly shaped from the force of whatever had shattered the bones beneath. Broken front teeth glimmered through the blood and meat of what had been her lips. But the face was still recognizable: Arleta Hocks.

No identification had been found on the woman, and Gebauer said he was pretty sure she had been killed elsewhere and dumped here. "The autopsy will verify it, but my guess is the body was pushed out of a car."

"Leads?"

He shook his head. "Nothing right off. We didn't see any knife or gun wounds—beating death probably. But by God she put up a fight. You can't see it because of the Baggies, but half the fingernails on her right hand were ripped back and the rest had shreds of skin under them. She clawed the hell out of somebody."

"Defense wounds?"

"Not evident—neither arm's broken. My guess is the killer

used his fists—it looks like somebody really lost it, Gabe. Just kept beating the shit out of her with his fists even after she was out or dead." He shook his head. "Fists wouldn't break the skin on her arms or shoulders, but the bruises'll show up on autopsy. My guess is they're there. I don't see how they couldn't be."

Wager did not spend much time at the crime scene. The victim was identified, there were no neighbors' doors to knock on, no witnesses standing and waiting to talk, no apartment windows overlooking the site. And the surrounding commercial buildings had been closed after five or six, their cleaning crews gone after eight. He interviewed the bearded and fragrant can collector who, pushing his shopping cart down the alley to scratch through the dumpsters, had found the body. He looked around the alley; a vehicle could have come in from only one of two entrances, probably the west where a quick right turn would take it out of its own lane without crossing traffic. If there had been any traffic late last night, and that's probably when her body was dumped, regardless of when she was killed.

Then Wager drove up Stout Street toward Mitchell Elementary School where Mrs. Hocks's two daughters should be.

The principal, a heavy woman whose brown eyes were enlarged by the thick lenses of her glasses, had shut the door to her office. "The Hocks girls? Their mother?"

"Yes, ma'am."

"Oh, Jesus. Lord Jesus. Poor children . . ."

"Yes, ma'am."

It had taken a good half hour before the girls, holding hands and wide-eyed with worry, were ushered into the principal's office. The school secretary had run a phone search for any relatives or close friends of the Hocks family, but it hadn't turned up anyone. Wager finally had to ask District Two to send a patrolman to knock on doors around the Hocks address for anyone who could come down and take the children home and look after them for a while. Social Services was notified, of course; and the school nurse, on duty that day at neighboring Harrington Elementary, was called over just in case. Wager, Mrs. Owings the principal, and a counselor, Mrs. Yankin, were waiting. The girls recognized him.

"Hello, Coley—how are you, Jeanette." There wasn't any easy way, and the pain and fear were already in their eyes. Wager knelt down to be level with them. "It's your mother, sweethearts. She was . . . in a bad accident." He shook his head, not wanting to say what he had to.

"She hurt?"

"I'm afraid she's dead, Coley. We're all very sorry."

"Dead? Mama?" The two girls wrapped their arms around each other and rigidly stared at him. "Dead?"

"You'll both be looked after, *queridas*. A neighbor's coming now to take you home, and we're calling your relatives in Texas."

Mrs. Owings's heavy arms folded around the two thin figures. "Oh, babies—you'll be all right. Sure you will!"

"I have to ask you some questions, Coley. You and Jeanette. Can you answer them for me?"

The older girl looked as if she didn't quite hear him or didn't understand what he was saying. Jeanette stared up at her sister, silent tears beginning to spill from her eyes.

"Coley, can you answer some questions for me? It will help me find out what happened."

The girl finally nodded. Short, black braids sprouted from her small head and wagged the polka-dotted ribbons tied at their ends.

"When did you see your mama last, sweetheart?"

"Yesterday. Afternoon. She . . . she found that book . . . she tried to call you and tell you and then she went into her room for a while. . . ."

"The book? The one John Erle was always writing in?"

"Yessuh. She axed me did I know where it was and I did. I know where John Erle liked to hide things. There's a board loose under his bed, like, and he put things there he didn't want us to know about. It was in there."

"That was after school yesterday?"

The girl nodded again, and her eyes wrenched with pain at the guilty thought that her action might have caused whatever happened.

Wager said quickly. "You did the right thing, sweetheart. Your mother asked you for it and you told her the truth—that was the right thing to do." Wager stroked the girl's shoulder like he would a frightened kitten. "She tried to call me?" The time on the memo had been, he thought, about five—late afternoon, anyway.

"Yessuh. Then she started reading in it and then she ran into her room for the longest time."

"What then, Coley?"

"We had us supper. It was late and Mama 'most burned the potatoes. She was, you know, real kind of worried-like. I axed her was anything wrong and she just looked at me like she didn't even know me. She made us go to bed early. Said we should ought to go to bed, and said it like she meant it. So's we did."

"Then what?"

"Nothing. We got up and come to school." She explained. "Lots of times she ain't home mornings. That's 'cause she got to work at the Seven-'Leven." The realization that her mother would never be home again came into her eyes, and the tears finally began.

"There now—" Mrs. Owings gathered both girls to her. "There, now—"

Wager persisted through the shaky gasps of both girls' wet breathing. "She wasn't home this morning?"

"No, suh."

He asked Mrs. Owings, "What time do the children arrive for school?"

"Eight forty-five. The first bell."

A four-, maybe five-block walk for the girls. "Do you know if your brother's book is still at home?"

Coley couldn't say anything, now. Her head wagged no, and now the crying started in earnest. Wager awkwardly patted both girls, their bony shoulders jerking and twitching under his palm. Then, leaving his business card for Mrs. Owings in case she needed anything from him, he got the hell out of there.

HE BROUGHT TWO uniformed patrolmen with him; one covered the rear of the house, the other two accompanied Wager to the front door. Bulky with his weapon, radio, and accoutrement belt, he and Wager almost filled the small front porch. The officer's heavy black shoe accidentally kicked a beer bottle across the boards, sending it off the porch with a hollow rattle. Wager banged on the doorframe with the side of his fist.

The notebook had not been found with the body; Wager, with a telephone warrant to establish the chain of evidence in case the notebook had to be used in court, found it at Mrs. Hocks's home. It was in the tiny room that served as her bedroom, sitting on a battered bureau that was missing some of its pull knobs. It was a small pocket notebook, bound with wire across the top and with bright green paper covers chapped and bent from riding in John Erle's pocket. Inside, in large and uneven writing, was the boy's schedule of his way to wealth: the plan he had for setting up his own drug ring, complete with a list of current prices, a roster of customers, actual or potential, and a page headed "BRs Rutine" and filled in with day, time, place, and initials that matched many of the names on the "List of Customers." You didn't have to be Sherlock Holmes to figure that John Erle had made a log of Big Ron's weekly business routine. Other pages held columns of numbers that showed that the boy had been shaving enough off his deliveries to develop a little stash of his own. A scrape here, a corner there, little enough so it wouldn't be noticed but, over time, it was building into a couple of ounces. Then there was the page that figured the margin—and where John Erle could place his ounce or two just under Big Ron's price but still make enough to build up his investment fund. He had the amounts carefully figured out and even the time schedule he intended to follow; prospective customers were listed, too, apparently those he thought could be trusted not to tell Big Ron that he was underselling. Another page had the names of half a dozen gangs, among them the L-102s and the word *Falcon* followed by the figure 25. That was probably the number of hits or ounces or chips he had promised to deliver when he finally got his route started.

It was a smart plan, workable and ambitious, and John Erle had been a sharp kid. He probably could have done it, too, if Big Ron hadn't somehow found out about it. A complaint about a light dime, maybe, or one of those names that the kid thought he could trust. What John Erle had not figured into his plan was that although Big Ron was stupid, he was also dangerous; that in the world he was entering, John Erle, no matter how much pluck, still needed luck. Because he had absolutely no value as a human being for anyone except his sisters and his mama.

Mrs. Tipton came to the door and didn't bother to glance at Wager's badge. "You again!" But the large woman's voice wasn't as strong as the last time Wager stood there. There was fear in it, and her eyes went nervously from Wager to the patrolman and back.

"Where's Big Ron, Mrs. Tipton? We've got a warrant for him."

"Why? What for?"

"Murder. He beat a woman to death."

"No!"

"Where is he?"

"He's my son—he wouldn't hurt nobody!"

"We both know that's a bunch of crap, lady. Open the door or we come in through it."

"You can't do that!"

"The hell we can't." The heel of Wager's fist banged the screen door and sent pieces of the lock clattering into the dim living room.

"You stop that—you can't do that!" She backed up quickly; one slipper flew off her foot as she pulled away from Wager, who lunged through the doorway.

He waved the folded S and S warrant in one hand and his pistol in the other; behind him, the uniformed officer stepped quickly into the dim living room and to the side of the door, his weapon out and searching for a target. Wager shoved the hefty cursing woman aside and went for the door that led from the living room deeper into the home. The gliding rustle of something moving in the dark warned him, and he flattened against the wall, shouting alert to the officer. "He's here!"

"No—he ain't! Ronnie—run—run, boy. They gonna kill you!"

"Jerry"—Wager keyed his radio—"he's coming out the back. Back door, Jerry!"

Three seconds later they heard a garbled shout from somewhere toward the rear of the home, then the pop of weapons, oddly soft and muffled, and, unconsciously, Wager counted them: one—two three—four five—six. Six shots, two weapons.

"Oh, my God! Ronnie—Ronnie!"

He pushed the struggling old lady out of his path to send her in a sprawl across the living room sofa, and sprinted for the back. The screen door stood open, snagged by a large twisted leg in cut-off jeans that twitched and jerked on the top step. Beyond that, across the small backyard and backed against the garage wall, Jerry Lindeman crouched in the two-handed delta position, his eyes stretched wide over the tilted and still smoking muzzle of his pistol. Wager froze, waiting until those eyes showed that Lindeman recognized Wager, then he came onto the back steps. Big Ron, grunting and doubled over, was grabbing at his chest with both fists; on the old sidewalk beyond his reach lay a chrome pistol. The side of the man's face had been bandaged, but his plunge down the worn plank steps and into the weeds beside the foundation had ripped the tape and cloth to reveal deep clawmarks across his cheek. It was as if he had been attacked by a crazed animal.

IT WAS WELL after dark by the time the paperwork was finished. Mrs. Tipton had been arrested for obstructing a peace officer, accessory to a crime, refusal to permit inspection, refusing to aid a peace officer, aiding escape, and compounding. Nonetheless, her lawyer had sprung her on bail in an hour or two, even while Wager was punished for doing his duty by having to complete the official forms. At least he had not been the one to shoot Big Ron, so that lengthy form, the shooting diagram, was not his to fill out.

Big Ron was alive—critical, but still alive, and Wager sent a memo to the DA's office that he thought the suspect had money hidden somewhere. Maybe the DA's financial crimes section could find it; no sense letting the state pay Big Ron's medical bills if the man had squirreled his profits away in his sock. Though he suspected that Mrs. Tipton was busy this very minute moving any cash or accounts to safer hiding.

She, of course, had made no statement other than to ask for her lawyer. But Wager had a pretty good idea what happened: Mrs. Hocks had seen in her son's book both the story of his corruption by Big Ron and the reason for Ron to kill her boy. It wasn't evidence that Wager could bring into court except as a probable motive, but it was enough to send the woman after Big Ron. Perhaps at first she asked, then accused, then attacked. And Ron reacted as he usually did by hitting out, and had kept hitting, even after she had stopped attacking him.

Ron had not made a statement either, sliding into shock

before they could get anything from him, and then being protected by his mother's lawyer before he was off the operating table. But Wager expected a self-defense plea—six-five and almost 300 pounds, Big Ron had been terrified of Mrs. Hocks, who had reached up and bit him in the shin for no reason and Your Honor Mr. Tipton swears he didn't mean to kill her, only to stop her from hurting him. Wager thought the best the state could do was murder in the second degree, a class 2 felony, and that's what he wrote for an initial charge. Tipton's lawyer would claim criminally negligent homicide, a class 1 misdemeanor. They would probably settle on a plea bargain for manslaughter, a class 4 felony with maybe two years to be served in prison on a four-year sentence. But when that hearing was over Wager would be ready to file the next case Big Ron and his lawyer would have to try and wiggle out of: premeditated murder. Because not only had Doty notified Wager that he found bloodstains matching Arleta Hocks's type on the underside of the trunk lid of the Cadillac belonging to Ron, but that the pistol Tipton had used to shoot at Officer Lindeman just happened to be a .32 caliber and just happened to match the slug that killed John Erle. Too dumb, too greedy, or both, Big Ron had kept the weapon he used to murder John Erle.

It wasn't worth what it had cost, but Mrs. Hocks would have her revenge after all, and Wager felt pretty damn good about that.

17

WHAT WAGER DIDN'T feel good about was the Neeley case and its unclear ties to Roderick Hastings. His mother used to tell him and his sisters that if you struggled, sooner or later the stone would break. Though she hadn't intended it that way, it was something any detective had to believe, too. But if you weren't even allowed to struggle, the stone stayed there, a rock in your shoe or a wall in your face. And it challenged your belief in your own abilities or in the very reasons behind the work you did. The thing that made it worse was the call from Aunt Louisa asking Wager if that reporter from the newspapers, Mr. Gargle, had talked to him about Julio.

"Not lately. What's the matter?"

The voice was shaky and muffled, coming through a nose still stuffed from crying. "He kept asking me if Julio had been selling narcotics. He kept saying that Julio was mixed up with a gang and that's why somebody shot him, because he was mixed up with narcotics."

"That's not true, Aunt Louisa. Gargan doesn't know what he's talking about."

"You're sure, Gabe? Really?"

"I'm positive. I don't know where he got that story, but it's a lie."

A long, quivering breath. "My son . . ."

Jesus. Maybe it would be better if mothers had no sons. "Don't you believe what that guy said, Aunt Louisa. Julio was a good kid."

"Yes."

"And I'm going to find out who killed him. Real soon, I promise you. And it will show that Julio didn't do what that reporter said."

"Yes."

After a few more words, she hung up, and Wager, knowing he shouldn't even as he jabbed at his telephone's number pad, called the editorial desk of the *Post*. Gargan was in.

"What the hell are you doing, Gargan, telling the mother of a homicide victim that her son was killed because he was dealing dope?"

"Hold it, Wager—just keep a civil tone in your head. I didn't tell her that. I asked her if it was true. She denied it."

"Goddamn right she denied it because it's not true! But you hurt the woman, Gargan. You made her think her dead son was a dirtbag."

"Hey, I got a story to write, and I was following my lead."

"What lead? Nobody ever told you Julio was dealing!"

"Oh, yeah! Yeah, they did, Wager. I interviewed the official officially in charge of the investigation—Officer Golding—and he made the statement that the killing seemed to be the result of a dealers' squabble. And that, Wager, is what I was following up on. If you've got further information pertaining to the case, I'd like to have your statement."

"My statement is go to hell, Gargan." As he was putting the receiver down, he heard the tiny voice say, "Hey, I hear you got shot. Too bad they—"

Golding wasn't at his desk; the location board said he was

on patrol. Wager reached him on the radio. "Where can we meet, Maury? And how soon?"

"The Satire? About half an hour?"

"I'll be there."

THE SATIRE LOUNGE on East Colfax was a favorite stop for old-timers in the department. It was owned by the brother of an ex-chief of police and offered a discount on meals for officers. Importantly, the cramped area where food was served was separate from the large barroom, so it didn't look like the cops were drinking on duty. Wager found Golding at one of the small booths beside the Colfax window, grazing on a large salad and sipping a cup of something.

"Gabe, what's the word?"

"I want to know why in the hell you told Gargan that Julio Lucero was a dealer."

The fork full of lettuce and purple onion slices hung in front of his chin, and Golding stared at him in surprise. "Because that's what I think!"

"On what evidence, Maury?"

"A statement from an informant. I been checking it out."

Wager studied the man's wide eyes. "Who? Who told you that?"

Golding put the forkful of greens into his mouth and chewed slowly. Then he washed it down with a sip from his cup. "Herb tea," he said. "Celestial Seasons chamomile. Soothes the nerves and lowers the blood pressure. Looks like you need some."

"I don't need any goddamned chamomile tea. Who told you that?"

"One of the people he worked with out at DIA. Davenport. Said the Lucero kid was selling dope out there."

Wager reached back in his memory. Freddy Davenport: white kid, late teens, scrawny goatee and moles. "Tell me about it."

"Well, that's just about it. He said he saw Lucero a couple times selling Shermans or speed or whatever to some of the construction workers. I figure he tried to skim a little and his supplier got pissed, or maybe he couldn't pay for a delivery for some reason." Another mouthful of lettuce and Golding talking around it. "I mean, it all fits: The kid's all of a sudden afraid, his mother says he's getting these phone calls that he won't answer. He's afraid to go outside. I figure somebody wanted him and they were watching his house, and when he went to the store—bang!—they got him."

It did make sense, and it wasn't an impossible story: John Erle had it happen to him. "So if he was dealing, what happened to his money? Dealers make money, but I haven't found anything saying Julio had any."

Golding shrugged. "Maybe he put it all up his nose."

"The autopsy doesn't show that. He was clean—no traces, no marks, no organ damage."

"OK. He was stashing it somewhere. He was smart enough to know that his mother would suspect him if he started flashing it around, so he put it somewhere." A final sip of tea. "It could be in a bank account, for all we know. Under a different name. Stay there till hell freezes over, now, and we'd never find it."

"His mother would find a record of it. A bankbook, a deposit slip, something."

"She looking for it?"

No. She wasn't, and Wager wasn't about to ask her to.

"She could have thrown it out by now, Gabe. Not even known what it was."

"Everybody knows what a bankbook is."

"OK. So maybe she knows and doesn't want to admit it. It wouldn't be the first time somebody covered for the dead—figure what difference does it make now, and destroy the evidence."

"She says he wasn't dealing. I believe her."

Golding watched his fork push some shreds of green pepper through a little pool of Italian dressing. "Well, she's not my relative, Gabe."

"What's that mean?"

"It means I've got to treat her just like anybody else. It means that I got to look at all the angles, not just the ones I would like to look at."

"Golding—"

"Hey, I'm not saying you would do it on purpose. But think about it, Gabe: You want to believe her. Her son was your cousin, she's your aunt, you've known her all your life, you want to believe her. Think about what that means."

Golding was right. He did want to believe Aunt Louisa. And when you started slanting your facts to fit what you wanted to believe, you could go way wrong on a case. Anybody could. "What else did Davenport say?"

"What do you mean?"

"About Julio's dealing. When did he see him do it? Who else saw it?"

"Nothing. Just that he saw it a couple times."

"He told you this when you went out to DIA?"

"No. Yesterday. He called me up and said he remembered it and thought I should know."

"Why didn't he tell you sooner?"

"I don't know. Didn't ask him. He just remembered, that's all. Witnesses do that, Gabe. You know that—that's why we leave our cards."

Wager knew it. He told Golding what he'd learned from LaBelle about Hastings.

"And Adamo confirmed it?"

"He'd heard there was a lot of action out there, but he didn't have any names."

"Jeez, that fits! I mean if Hastings maybe has something going out there, and here's Lucero working with or for him, right? Or maybe he's even moving in on Hastings's territory. That's a whole nother angle, Gabe!"

It was, and whichever angle you looked from, it was ugly. He might know in his heart that Julio wasn't involved in dealing, but Arleta Hocks had felt the same way about John Erle. In fact, the shock of reading that little book and finally seeing the truth was what had made her crazy enough to look for Big Ron.

Golding was counting out a couple of ones and some change to cover his meal. "I'll get on that, Gabe. Anything else you've come up with?"

"No. Nothing else."

DEWING HAD ORDERED him, if he cared for his job, to stay as far as possible from any contact with Neeley or anyone who knew the man. But as much as Wager did care, he had made a promise to Aunt Louisa and that was all there was to it. A short call to the Motor Vehicle Division for a name on Roderick Hastings's license plate told him that the car was registered to a Harold Allen and had been bought less than six months ago. Previous owner: Sunrise Motors on East Colfax in Aurora. That figured. That dealership was known in area police departments as one that made a lot of money recycling cars through various gang members. If a car was wanted for a particular job, a member would buy it under a false name, use it for a few days, and then sell it back to the dealer for 20 percent less than the original cost, plus repairs. It was a good deal all around. It provided an unlimited and varied supply of legitimate and untraceable cars, it saved the gangsters a bundle in overhead, it gave a nice, steady income to the dealer, and—except for the false registration—it was perfectly legal. And as for the little question of the registration, hey, the guy came in and said that's who he was and where he lived; no law says a dealer has to check an ID before selling a car. A joke around the department was that

Sunrise Motors was the only dealership that washed your car and wiped it clean of prints, too.

As for Freddy Davenport, nowhere had Wager found any indication that he was connected to Neeley, Hastings, Heisterman, or any of the various Bloods gangs. A search through CCIC and NCIC had not turned up any figure who matched the kid with the skinny goatee, and no one Wager asked had ever heard of him. So Davenport was not only clean enough to keep Dewing happy, he was fair game, and Wager went after him.

IT DIDN'T TAKE long, MVD's file listed only one Freddy with a birth date that matched this one's age; his home address was on Acoma Street in the Platte Park neighborhood of south Denver. Wager parked directly in front of the frame house with its porch and front door tacked awkwardly like a small box to a corner of the building. When Davenport drove up from work, Wager watched the youth back into the parking place Wager left in front of him. The frame around the license plate said TIGHT BUNS DRIVE ME NUTS and the vanity plate itself said REDY-1. Ready Freddy. Maybe it paid to advertise. Lunch box in hand, Davenport started across the lawn toward his front door.

Wager stepped out of his car. "Hello, Freddy. Got a minute?"

"Oh—hi." He looked puzzled, trying to place Wager. "Where'd we meet?"

"Out at DIA. I asked you a couple questions about Julio Lucero."

"Oh, yeah! Right—you're the—" He stopped in midsentence as he thought of something. Looking suddenly uncomfortable, he asked, "I mean, how's it going?"

"Fine, fine. Have you remembered anything that might help me find Julio's killer?"

"No! I would've called you, man. I still got your card." His

free hand patted at his shirt pocket and then his hip pocket.
"Somewhere."

Wager nodded. "I'm glad to hear that. How are you and
Roderick Hastings getting along?"

"Rod? OK—I mean, we only see each other on the job,
so . . . why?"

"He's deep in shit, Freddy. He's going to go under real soon,
and so is anybody with him."

"I'm not . . . I don't know what you mean, man."

"Anybody working with him, anybody doing what he's doing—they're called accessories, and they get the same treatment."

"Hey, I don't know what the guy's into, man. I mean it's not
like we're big buddies or something. I only see him on the job,
and the job's only got another few weeks to go—another couple
paydays, that's it, and then I probably won't never see the guy
again!"

Wager studied the youth's light blue eyes, looking for guile
or excessive innocence or that blankness used by a lot of people
to convince themselves that they're not lying. But all he saw was
worry. "I talked to Detective Golding a couple hours ago,
Freddy. He told me what you reported about Julio. That he was
selling dope to construction workers out at DIA."

His thumb scratched in the little tuft of brown hairs at the
tip of his chin. "Yeah—ah—I mean that's maybe what I thought
I saw. I mean maybe that wasn't it, you know?"

"No. I don't know. You tell me exactly what you saw."

"Ah, well, I mean maybe he was just talking to these guys,
like. I mean it looked like he was handing them something, but
maybe I was wrong."

"When, where, and who, Freddy? Tell me now. Exactly.
Where were you standing, where was Julio standing, exactly
what did you see?"

"Aw, man!"

"It was a lie, wasn't it, Freddy? You never saw Julio deal a thing, did you?"

"Aw—"

"Why? Are you working with Hastings?"

"Naw, man. I don't know nothing about Hastings." He winced and twisted his torso as if his shirt itched and then said, "Aw shit, look, it was just a joke, like. Hastings saw that story on you and Julio in the newspaper. You know, the one told about Julio being your cousin and all . . . ."

"Go on."

"Well, he said it would be funny to sort of, you know, make it look like a cop's relative was dealing. You know, embarrass a cop—a practical joke, like."

"Why didn't he call Golding himself?"

"I don't know. He said it would sound better coming from me—coming from a white guy. It was just a joke, man!"

"So you made a false report."

"It was a joke!"

"What do you know about Hastings dealing?"

"Rod?" Davenport's surprise looked genuine. "I . . . I don't . . . I never thought of it. . . ."

"You've never seen Hastings do anything that looked like he was selling dope to the construction workers?"

"No." He shook his head for emphasis. "The guy's not around that much—he's always cutting out."

"What do you mean?"

"He leaves. Tarbell's got a schedule, like. Gets us going and checks once around noon, and then in the afternoon. Rod takes off for about a half hour, always gets back before Tarbell shows up again."

"Where does he go?"

"Says he takes a crap—got some kind of stomach trouble, he says. Says for us not to tell Tarbell so he won't get fired. But he does his work—I mean he makes up for it when he gets back, so as long as he does his share, we don't care."

"He does this every day?"

"Yeah, midmorning, midafternoon. Says he can't go more than three hours without taking a crap. Some kind of bug he got in the service, he said."

The only service Hastings saw was slinging hash at the state pen cafeteria. But with regular meets, say near the portable toilets, making sales twice a day every day, the man could distribute a hell of a lot of drugs and make a hell of a lot of money. One, two thousand a day? No problem. Maybe more than that, if he sold enough. Fifteen, twenty thousand a week was a good estimate. It was a lot of pocket change.

"Is it possible that Julio saw Hastings dealing?"

"I don't know. Could've. He was always being sent here or there for—" The meaning of Wager's question finally reached his brain. "Oh, shit."

A lot of pocket change. Enough to shoot a kid for, if that kid somehow was a threat to take it away.

"Oh, man. Hey, honest to God I didn't never think of . . ."

"You know what the penalty is for a false report?"

"What? No."

"It's not that much. Just a class-one petty crime—most you can get is a five hundred dollar fine and six months in county jail."

"Man, listen—I just did it for a joke, man! I had no idea none of this other stuff was going on, even!"

"But the thing is, Freddy, I'll bet some of Hastings's bros are sitting in the county jail, too. They hang out a lot in places like that, you know? And they're the kind who'd be happy to do him a favor. They like tight buns. Especially on a nice tender white boy who says he's ready."

"Aw, come on, man—"

"You tell me the truth, Davenport, you tell it right now and I'll help you out. You lie and I will toss you into the Denver

County jail like dog meat. Now: Are you dealing dope with Hastings?"

"No!" Again he shook his head. "I swear! I swear to God!"

Wager peered into the youth's eyes, wondering what it was about the color blue that made them more difficult to read. "Today was your last day at work, Freddy. You just quit."

"No problem. What you tell me about Hastings maybe doing what he did to Julio, no problem, man!" He added, "There's only two or three weeks of work left, anyway."

"You don't call Hastings, you don't see him, you don't talk to him."

"I don't even know where he lives, man—we never get together after work, and I don't want to!"

"And not another word to anyone about Julio dealing."

"Oh, no. Not a word . . . Listen, Officer, I'm sorry about that, you know? It was a dumb thing to do and I'm really sorry. I mean that."

"I hope I don't have to talk to you again, Freddy."

"No! I mean, me too. I mean, yeah, you won't. Believe me!"

He left the youth leaning weakly on the fender of his parked car, sweating and sagging as if he'd run a long distance on a hot day. But Wager's mind wasn't on Davenport: it was on a part of their conversation—the part that finally clicked in with that tangle of ideas he had been unraveling just before the dispatcher sent him to Arleta Hocks's corpse.

18

WHY WOULD HASTINGS want Golding to think that
Julio had been dealing? Why draw attention to it at all? Time.
If every day meant another couple of thousand dollars, and every
week another fifteen or twenty thousand, then what Hastings
wanted was time. Especially if the construction was going to
begin shutting down in a couple weeks. Time enough to hang
on for those last few weeks, for that last thirty or forty thousand
dollars. Maybe if the airport job was just starting or had another
year or two to go, Hastings would not have bothered to hurt Julio,
just pulled out and come back later. Maybe. But there was something about wanting that last little bit that sharpened a greedy
person's hunger. And dope pushers weren't in the business for
charity. Besides, Julio—like John Erle—was a nobody. A
throwaway.

Wager sat at the keyboard of his computer waiting for the
CCIC to open up for him. It had been twenty minutes since he
sent in his request, and the system was still backed up by other
traffic. So he waited. He could have gone on to the other paperwork that was stuffed into his pigeonhole, but he would have
had trouble focusing on it. So he just sat there, glancing at the

screen's "Please Wait" now and then, staring at the office wall betweentimes.

It really had been a chess game. Or checkers. Or whatever. A game, anyway, whose rules and aims had been hidden from him and only the effects of someone else's moves felt. But Hastings finally screwed up. Trying to muddy the water one more time in order to be certain of that last couple of weeks, he had used Davenport to call Golding instead of doing it himself. Wager could see it now, the man wondering how close Wager was getting as he probed into Julio's death; knowing from the rumors and phone calls that Wager was constantly poking, looking, asking. Then, from Gargan's news story, Hastings learned why: He or one of his people had killed a cop's cousin. And all Hastings wanted was a few weeks more. Just hold Wager off for those few weeks . . . First, try it through a very willing Neeley and his bullshit suit to give Wager something else to think about. Then add a witness—Nelda Stinney—in case Wager wasn't taking Neeley's charges seriously enough. Hide behind Davenport to feed a line of crap to Golding, knowing it would get back to Wager . . . But Hastings finally screwed up with that move. He screwed up because Davenport had no ties to the Neeley case, and that had allowed Wager to move in close enough.

Now Wager felt impatience, the kind that always came when things started falling together and he began to understand. When at least he got an answer from the CCIC, it wasn't surprise but confirmation that he felt, and a twinge of self-contempt: He could have known it all along, but it wasn't until his conversation with Davenport that he gave himself the clue. It should have been something he thought of much sooner.

There was indeed a Stinney in Cañon City, but it wasn't Nelda: first name Wayne, middle initial R., a Department of Corrections number, as well as a Denver Police Department number. Wager printed out the information and pushed back from his desk with a sigh. Then he took the elevator to Records.

Wayne Russell Stinney. Wager read down the vitals until he came to "Spouse." Nelda. And her address was still that grimy apartment building where Neeley had tried to kill Wager with a shotgun. Maybe, in fact, that was why Neeley had run into that building in the first place—looking for Nelda's apartment, a bed to crawl under, someone to tell Wager that the guy he was chasing wasn't there. And that was how Heisterman knew to locate his so-called witness. Maybe the lawyer even came up with the idea. Maybe not—more likely it was Hastings's inspiration: a way to get Julio's cousin off their backs long enough to finish out the job at DIA. A phone call to Neeley, who would be real happy to file a suit; a warning to Nelda, either she testified that she saw Wager shoot an unarmed Neeley or her old man would never leave Cañon City alive. The gang ties—Neeley, Heisterman—all led to Hastings and to his hunger for just a few more weeks of profit. Wager should have seen it sooner, but even with that thought, he felt a massive lightening of spirit, a fading of the worry about Neeley that had been with him even while he slept, even while he tried to pretend that it wasn't there.

He ran off a copy of Stinney's sheet and went back to his desk to call Attorney Dewing.

"I told you to stay away from anybody associated with the case, Detective Wager!"

"Counselor, I haven't talked to anybody who knows Neeley. This is from open records. Nelda Stinney is lying to save her husband."

"I think we'd better meet. Bring that with you."

"IT'S A GOOD story."

They sat in the same booth at Dewing's favorite restaurant, but this time Wager didn't have a salad; it was after hours, he was off duty, and he was thirsty. His second beer sat half-drained on the tiny paper napkin in front of him. Counselor

Dewing was still working on her first glass of white wine. "But not strong enough for a dismissal, that what you mean?"

She nodded, short hair swinging past her ears. "If Nelda went to the judge and said she was coerced into testifying falsely, Neeley's charges would be out—no question—and Neeley or whoever would be up for intimidating a witness. But it's not likely she's going to do that, is it? So we have to wait until she takes the stand and then bring this out on cross-examination." She explained, "We'll let her make her false statement, then tell her what perjury is and what penalties she's subject to, and give her a chance to save her butt by retracting."

"And if she sticks to it?"

"We use this information to reduce her credibility—we show the judge that Neeley has something to gain by lying."

Wager considered that. "It doesn't put my hands on Hastings, though. He's the one I'm after."

"What you're after right now is protecting your career. What we have here"—she tapped the printout—"is only one argument for your innocence, not incontestable proof of it, so this doesn't get you off the hook. Besides, Hastings isn't even your case."

"He's mine, all right, Counselor. Just not officially."

"Detective Wager—"

"Right. Don't go near him."

"Don't. For your own sake." She shrugged. "After we clear you, you can chase him from here to China if you want to. But prior to that . . ."

Wager smiled agreement. "All right." They talked some more about tactics and Heisterman, what the lawyer would probably do to protect Stinney and what they could do to make her vulnerable. But Wager's mind wasn't really on that issue, and Dewing finally noticed it.

"Do I get the feeling I don't have your undivided attention, Detective Wager?"

"It's divided, Counselor," Wager said. "But I hear your every word."

"It's your career." There was a warning shrug in her voice.

"And my life," he agreed. But his mind was still on Hastings and on playing a different game. His own game this time, one that might lead Hastings into an even bigger mistake.

WAGER BEGAN MAKING his moves as soon as he left Dewing. He didn't tell the attorney all that he was going to do; it would have just interfered with her concentration on his case. But as he had told her, the issue was not only his career but also his life—and if the two conflicted, well, it was himself he had to live with. And that, he sighed, included his family.

Weaving across town through the heavy, quitting-time traffic, he swung off Park Avenue onto Washington, slowing as he approached 16th Avenue. The curbs were jammed with cars that had no garages; he had to pull into a space marked NO PARKING FROM HERE TO CORNER. Flipping down the car's visor to show the police card, he walked up the heavily carpeted hallway to Hastings's apartment.

The massive figure with the upright sheaf of woolly hair opened the door again. "Is Roderick Hastings here?" asked Wager.

"No."

"You're Kwame Mitchell?"

"Yeah."

"Mind answering a couple questions?" He folded his badge case away.

The broad shoulders lifted and fell, but the man said nothing.

"Can you tell me where you were a week ago Tuesday— about midnight."

"Why?"

"Somebody shot at me."

The hooded, dark eyes gazed down at Wager. "Why would I shoot at you?"

"Could have been Roderick. Either way—" He was interrupted by a pop from his radio and a familiar voice calling his number. "Excuse me a minute, OK?" Wager waited until the sprouts of hair on the man's large head bobbed affirmative. Then he stepped away from the door to mutter into the radio. "Go ahead, Maury."

"That call you've been waiting for—it came through. He says he'll meet with you later tonight."

Wager glanced at the large man who leaned against the doorsill, his head bent slightly so his upright hair wouldn't brush the lintel. "What time?" He turned away from Mitchell's nosy stare and big ears.

"Twelve-thirty."

"Twelve-thirty tonight?"

"That's affirmative."

"All right. Where?"

"Valverde Park. Be alone, he says."

"Valverde. On the west side. Right. Hell of a place to meet."

"He's a shy type."

"With reason. Thanks, Maury."

He clicked his radio off and slipped it back into its belt carrier. "Sorry about that." He smiled up at Mitchell. "Always business."

"I got business, too."

"This won't take long. Just tell me where you were."

"Here. Sleep."

"Any witnesses?"

"To watch me sleep? Shit, man, you a fool?"

"What about Hastings? Doesn't he live here too?"

"Uh-huh."

"But he wasn't here, so he can't swear you were asleep?"

He saw Wager's trick, and quick anger lit the man's dark eyes. "He was here. I was here. We was both here." He added, "And you can't prove we wasn't!"

Wager smiled. "Somebody always sees something, Ball Peen. And somebody is always willing to talk for the right price. I'll be around again."

Mitchell, face taut with dislike, pushed the heavy door shut with a thud.

LABELLE RHONE'S VOICE rose in pitch. "You want me to what?"

"Just tell him what I told you. That's all."

"Why in hell should I tell him anything? Or do you no favors neither?"

"Because you have nothing to lose, and either way you're going to be happy."

The line was silent for a long minute. Then, "You want me to tell him you gonna meet with a informant who knows who killed . . . What was his name?"

"Julio. Julio Lucero."

"A informant who knows who killed Julio and who knows all about why he was killed."

"And that you heard it—"

"And that I heard you talking about it over some radio while you was talking to me about that fight over at JP's."

"That's all you have to tell him. I'll take care of the rest."

"Or he'll take care of you."

"Like I said, LaBelle. You win either way."

"Yeah."

Not that Hastings would trust her. He'd check out her story. But Wager had made enough of a trail at JP's Lounge, talking to witnesses whose names Andy Powers had given him, to convince Hastings that there was some truth to what LaBelle said.

Enough, anyway, that he couldn't ignore it. And then he and his partner Ball Peen would talk about what they could do, and—which would keep Counselor Dewing happy—Wager would not have to approach them. They would come to him.

VALVERDE PARK WAS a small patch of worn grass that had a few trees and the usual playground equipment that had seen high use and low maintenance. In the dark, its size increased, and the shadows were made blacker by the streetlights surrounding the open stretch. Most of the lights in the homes were off by now, and Wager could hear—carried on the damp air of night—the grunt and rattle of a switch engine working the sidings in the distant Platte Valley yards. Slouched behind the wheel of his unmarked police car, his shape was a faint congealing of the darkness, dimly outlined through the window by the streetglow.

He had not told Elizabeth exactly where he was going, but it had been enough to live up to his promise to her. "I have to meet a guy—an informant."

She looked up over the tops of her glasses. "Like that last time?"

"No way will it be like the last time."

"But it's dangerous?"

He shook his head. "Not really. Just a meeting." They were only a few days from the election, and with the close race against Dennis Trotter, she had enough on her mind.

Wager glanced at the dim green pips of his watch: ten after midnight. Elizabeth was probably finishing up tonight's neighborhood meet-the-candidates gathering about now; starting home in a few minutes. He'd promised to call her after this little adventure. If it didn't take too much time, maybe he'd even drop by. All he'd had time to tell her over the phone was that he had some good news about the Neeley charges; she'd been heading out the door for her meeting, and he'd had a few things to take care of, too, so the call was brief. But she sounded almost as happy as he had felt and wanted to know more as soon as he could tell her.

So his mind was on that, though his ears were open for the sound of approaching feet, and his eyes watched the slide of each pair of headlights that crossed through the darkness of the small park. But the approaching, dark-clad figure moved almost soundlessly, and Wager didn't hear anything until the muffled scrape of soft rubber soles on a gritty curb turned his head. The rider's side—he was looming at the rider's side again and then the night split into the orange-red spray of a shotgun blast—two, three of the hollow explosions and the ripping, slapping sound of lead thudding into the slouched figure.

Wager braced his arm on the parked car's still warm hood. "Police—surrender!" And fired. The automatic bucked quickly twice. The flash of the first round showed him where to place the second. The figure with the shotgun swore and ran toward the park, pumping and firing as it ran, and Wager shot again, keeping his rounds low so they would not carry across the open space toward the dark homes beyond.

"Goddamn!" The figure tumbled, still firing. "Help me, BP—give me some cover, man!"

A second dark-clad figure stirred in a pool of shadow ten yards from where Wager crouched, and the hot, flashing glare of the automatic weapon shoved him up against the car. The vehicle quivered like a living thing as rounds punched into it, and Wager could smell the sudden, pungent odor of spilling gasoline. The MP-5 sprayed again, glass shattering in chips and beads and stinging Wager's hand that gave thin shelter to his face and eyes. Orange sparks of glowing steel bounced like angry fireflies across the asphalt. The car lurched again and then rose off its springs with a lung-pressing roar as the gasoline torched into a sheet of yellow-blue flames. Wager, rolling frantically from the billow of exploding fumes, tried to scramble to the safety of darkness, but the crack and whine of slugs ripped through the roaring glare of the fire, and he did not think he would make it.

Crawling, rolling, slapping at the flame that whipped like a hot flag from his coat sleeve, he heard the high-pitched crack of a rifle, then a second round, then the rattle and flash of the automatic weapon stopped and there was only the deep, windy roar of the flaming car.

WAGER, NOSTRILS PINCHED against the smell of gas fumes, the stink of burned cloth and hot metal, the mix of oil and steam from the still-smoking car, stared at the pillows that had been wrapped in a blanket and placed behind the wheel of his vehicle to look like a slouching man. Golding, carrying the .308 rifle with its laser scope, peered in through the other window.

"Lord, Gabe. He would have really had your ass this time!"

The hard glare of searchlights from the clattering firetrucks washed out the erratic red-white-blue flash of surrounding police vehicles and made the shredded holes in the blanket look almost colorless. The scorch of gunpowder showed up as dark smudges, and through the holes, spongy wads of filling looked vaguely like torn flesh. "Ball Peen came damn close to it with that MP-five. What the hell took you so long?"

"He was running toward you and shooting. It's harder than hell to keep that laser dot on a running target. I don't care what they tell you on the range." He added, "I'm sorry about it, though. Really."

"OK, Maury, no harm done." Not to Wager, anyway. Ball Peen was dead: the .308 elk round had ripped through his lungs and heart and put him in the dirt where he belonged. Hastings was only wounded—once in the side and once in the knee.

Screaming first for a doctor and then for his lawyer even as the ambulance attendants loaded him up. And, of course, two police cars suffered a little damage—Wager's from bullets and Golding's from burning up. Chief Doyle would not be overjoyed when that report landed on his desk in the morning. But Wager was damned if he was going to use his own car to stop any more bullets; his insurance was high enough. "You made a good shot, Maury. I'm glad I'm here to thank you."

"Yeah, well . . ." Golding shrugged modestly. "Maybe I should eat more carrots for my night vision."

They watched the gurney with its rubber sheet rattle past on its way to the second ambulance.

Golding wagged his head. "You were right, Gabe. Hastings was the kind of guy who just couldn't quit when he was ahead."

Wager, thinking more of Julio, of Arleta Hocks, than of Hastings or Ball Peen, said, "Yeah."

Golding started unscrewing the night scope from the rifle. "You think Hastings will cop to killing Julio?"

"What's he have to gain? We'll have to argue circumstantial evidence on that one—motive and opportunity." But tonight's criminal attempt at murder was a class-three felony, and even Heisterman wouldn't be able to get Hastings off the hook on this one. And Wager—Kolagny or no—would make sure all the aggravating circumstances, including Julio's death, were aired at the sentencing. It wasn't the nice, neat ending you got on those TV detective shows, and the paperwork for tonight's fun and games was just beginning, but Wager was satisfied.

Golding gently placed the scope in its case and stared for a long moment at the blasted pillows in Wager's car. "I was thinking it's too bad the Lucero kid can't come back and testify. But"—he wagged a thumb at the torn pillows—"in a way you did. I mean, Hastings must have thought you were gone, Gabe."

Wager nodded. He was thinking of Elizabeth, too, and wondering if it was too late to call her. Maybe not. Maybe she would be still awake, worried and anxious to hear from him. In fact, he was certain she was.

"Speaking of which, I read about this guy lives up in the mountains behind Boulder. He's into cryogenics. You know, freezing a body until science comes up with a cure for what killed it." He snapped the locks on the scope and hoisted the .308 to his shoulder like a successful hunter coming down from the hills. "He has his own grandfather on ice. Wouldn't that be something? Be able to bring a member of your family back from the dead?"